HIGGLEDY PIGGLEDY

HIGGLEDY PIGGLEDY

ROBIN SKELTON

**PULP
PRESS**

VANCOUVER

For William David Thomas, who tells a good tale.

HIGGLEDY PIGGLEDY
Copyright © 1992 by Robin Skelton

Published by
PULP PRESS
Arsenal Pulp Press Ltd.
100-1062 Homer Street
Vancouver, B.C.
Canada V6B 2W9

The Publisher gratefully acknowledges the ongoing assistance of The Canada Council and The Cultural Services Branch, B.C. Ministry of Tourism and Culture.

Typeset by the Vancouver Desktop Publishing Centre
Printed by Kromar Printing
Printed and bound in Canada

CANADIAN CATALOGUING IN PUBLICATION DATA:
Skelton, Robin, 1925-
 Higgledy piggledy

 ISBN 0-88978-247-4

 I. Title.
PS8537.K44H5 1992   C813'.54   C92-091089-0
PR9199.S44H5 1992

76982

CONTENTS

Higgledy Piggledy

I WAS ONCE CURSED WITH A HEN. Not by a hen, you understand, but with one. It was a black hen, the only black hen in our chicken run back of the house, if you could call it a chicken run. I mean, it was simply an enclosure of stakes and chickenwire, rather imperfectly put together, because I put it together myself and I'm no handyman at all. As a consequence of my limitations the chickens were always getting out and roaming around the vegetable plot and pecking in the flower beds, and even scratching around near the back door, but at least they were easy to get to go into their hut at night. They were, you may say, biddable, even the rooster.

My wife and I really enjoyed having the chickens. They may not be the most intelligent creatures in the world, but they are good providers. Ours provided us with eggs at a great rate, and no hen was more productive than the black one. I don't really understand these things—maybe it's something to do with hormones—but that black hen laid eggs as if her second name was Guinness. In fact we called her our Guinness Hen, which confused the neighbours who thought we meant Guinea Hen, and suspected us of being unable to distinguish between feathered varieties. One friend pointing at a crow on the back fence, even asked us if that was our peacock. Still, there we were, happy little chicken farmers, if a dozen or so fowl entitles us to the lable.

It was a lazy life, I must admit. Well, both of us were retired, and we saw no reason to do anything we didn't find pleasurable. We investigated the village a couple of miles down the road, patronized the local store, bought bric-a-brac and bits of furniture at what called itself The Antique Shoppe, and on fine days we'd picnic either by the river, or in the old graveyard overlooking it. It was so quiet and restful there under the trees.

It was in May that the difficulties began. At first it was rather amusing. Our Guinness Hen was the cause of our amusement. She would scuttle into the kitchen and, believe it or not, attack the cat. The cat rarely stayed around. I sometimes think he felt it a just retribution for all the smaller birds he had slaughtered when young. Certainly this particular bird was too big for him. Having defeated the cat, Guinness (we called her that for short) would leave evidence of bowel excitement on the floor, which was a nuisance, but one has to pay for one's entertainment.

After a few days we became a little irritated. The cat was becoming neurotic, and would peer round the kitchen door before coming in, and at the slightest sound of a scratch at the door he would disappear. Oh yes, that hen scratched at the door to be let in, as if it were a Christian—if I dare use that expression. Still, it was becoming less of an amusement than an affliction, and so we stopped opening the door for the hen. It made little difference, though. As soon as we opened the door for some other reason, she would scuttle in. We attempted to catch her and expel her, but she showed a surprising turn of speed, and on more than one occasion scuttled into other parts of the house. Moreover she could fly—not far or high—but far enough and high enough to get onto tables and even cupboards. One day she flew onto the welsh dresser and dislodged several pieces of Crown Derby which crashed into smithereens. We tried to shrug it off, but when, a day or two later, she made it onto an occasional table and destroyed a reputedly Ming vase we had picked up at the antique store, we were very angry. We told each other that she was for the pot, but no sooner had we said this than she charmed us by squatting on the hearthrug in the living room, and with a loud squawk, deposited a big brown egg. It almost seemed like an apology. So we didn't try to wring her neck—as a matter of fact we wouldn't have known how to do it anyway—we simply moved breakables out of her flight range, and shut doors behind us, as if we had a small rambunctious child in the house. And that hen was in the house a good deal of time. We took to opening the back door cautiously, and shooing her from her waiting position, but that was a hard hen to stop. Indeed, the result of our caution was only that a black head would poke through the gap between door and doorpost and deliver a sharp peck at the nearest ankle. We took to wearing rubber boots when we went out that way, even though the weather was warm.

The strategy worked for only a few days, and then Guinness took to using the windows, which we liked to keep open in mild weather. We had to close them. It did not deter her. She used the door we had cut for the cat. We nailed it shut. There was no point in retaining it; the cat had left home and taken up residence with the owner of the antique shop. We saw him there, but we did not reclaim him. I don't think he wanted to be reclaimed, for as soon as we entered the shop and saw him curled up cosily on a tapestry cushion in a reputedly Jacobean chair, he uncurled and departed with rapidity.

It was all beginning to get to us. We felt we were under siege. The siege's biggest guns, however, had yet to commence their barrage. It was on a Sunday morning, and as I went downstairs to make the tea I trod on something which went "crack" and discovered I had stepped on an egg. It was not as easy as you might think to remove a broken egg from a wool shag carpet. Later, my wife trod on another one in the living room. We took to walking around the house with our heads bent as if we belonged to some penitential order of medieval monks. We were sure who was responsible. We had stopped calling her Guinness though in fact she clearly deserved to be in the Book of Records under some heading or other; we simply referred to her as The Hen, or, more emphatically, That Hen.

That Hen practically dominated our lives. One morning we went out for a picnic lunch in the old graveyard, and when we returned we discovered the house had been invaded. There were hens everywhere. On the tables, on the chairs, in the closets. One was even squatting and clucking in the bath. That Hen, however, was nowhere to be seen. We opened the back door and a good deal of shouting, shooing and prodding with the broom the antique shop had sold us as a bygone, was needed. Two took refuge under the sofa where they left copious signs of their agitation. One sat on a cupboard and would not come down.

"Call the police," yelped my wife hysterically.

I said, "There isn't one—I mean there aren't any."

"Phone someone!" gasped my wife, as she crept up on a hen hiding behind an armchair. I didn't know who to call.

"The SPCA," she suggested in a squeak. The cord on the phone had been bitten, or rather pecked through.

When at last we had got them all out, counted them and recounted, we looked around for the black hen. She, we were certain, must have been the ring leader. There she was, perched on an upturned wheelbarrow, looking as sleepy and innocent as only a hen can. I swore loudly. We went inside. "But how?" I said. My wife, shaking, pointed at the broken milk-bottles with their attendant lake of milk by the back door.

"Joe slipped them inside to keep them out of the sun," she told me, "and he didn't latch the door behind him." I supposed she was right, but I was beginning to think that such a simple obstacle as a latched door would be unlikely to defeat the ingenuity of That Hen.

The breaking point came two days later, or I should say nights. I woke out of a deep sleep around dawn and there at my feet on the rail of our (reputedly Victorian) brass bed That Hen was roosting comfortably.

As I gaped, she opened her eyes and gave me a bright yellow stare of triumph. Then, almost leisurely, she flopped forward onto the bed, and before my horrified eyes she calmly laid an egg. I was practically paralysed, and totally devoid of coherent speech. I gave my wife a sharp nudge in the ribs.

"Whhhaaa?" she enquired, "Whaa?" and then she saw the bird, and produced a noise halfway between a strangled cry and a whistle and pulled the bedclothes up over her head. That Hen looked at me and I at her. She smiled. I swear she smiled. And then with great deliberation she gave the egg a peck like a pickaxe and it broke all over our (possibly Georgian) patchwork quilt. I leapt from bed with a roar, but she was too quick for me. She was out of the room and half way down the stairs before I had reached the top step, from which I fell.

"You were lucky you didn't break something," said the Doctor later that day. "But all you really need is a bit of rest. Put your feet up."

I said, "I wish I could, but we promised a friend from the village that we'd take her out to lunch at our favourite picnic place."

"Where's that?" enquired the Doctor idly.

"The old graveyard overlooking the river."

He was just picking up his bag, but he stopped. He said casually, "Which part of it?"

"Under the trees at the south end."

He sat down on the edge of the bed. "That's a bit unwise," he told me. "It's not a good place."

"Why ever not?" He hesitated, then he noticed the patchwork quilt in a heap on the floor, the egg stain showing clearly.

"What happened?" he said, gesturing.

"Well, we have a . . . hen . . . a black hen . . . and it . . . she . . . sometimes gets in."

"It terrorizes us," my wife sobbed, "it simply terrorizes us. It's worse than the . . . Mongol Hordes."

"Ahhh," said the Doctor, "that explains it. The southside of the graveyard, eh!"

"What's that got to do with it?" I asked sharply. He rubbed his chin.

"I'm supposed to be a man of science," he said, "but I've lived around these parts quite a while so maybe I'm not quite as scientific as I used to be. A while ago, sixty or so years, someone was buried there. It's a big flat gravestone. There's no moss or lichen on it Maybe you've noticed it?"

We said we had.

"Well," he said, "if I were you I would go on your picnic, and I would put a pretty bunch of flowers on that grave, and, if you can bear to do it, I would suggest you apologize for the past intrusions and promise you won't intrude again. Then take your picnic down by the river."

"You mean . . .?" said my wife, relief and incredulity combining in her tone.

"I am not going to say any more," said the Doctor, "but that is my prescription for what, er, ails you." He turned to the door.

"But a hen!" I said, "It was, I mean . . . a *hen*."

The Doctor gave a sly smile. "You should be thankful," he said. "Last time this happened it was a bear."

The Key

I T WAS A DREAM, OF COURSE.
I knew it as soon as I got inside the bookshop. The shelves were all curved for one thing—I don't mean bent, I mean curved like a bay window, and all the books were bound in leather, old leather. They looked eighteenth century or seventeenth century to me. Well, knowing how quickly dreams shift their ground, I decided I might not have much time to look the books over, so I reached out and took one from the shelf. Usually, when this happens in my dreams the words don't make much sense, or they jumble and vanish as I look at them. This time they stayed on the page and I could read them. I was astonished at my luck. The text, however, was not particularly interesting. It was a volume of sermons. Who needs sermons? I put that book back and took out another. It didn't change to something else in my hands, as I'd half expected, and I held my breath as I opened it. The title page said simply 'A Guide', it didn't say to where or to what. I was just turning the page when I became aware that someone was looking at the book over my shoulder. I turned on my heel.

It wasn't a woman I had seen before, or even a mixture of women I'd known, as dream figures often are. It was an entirely new personality. Moreover, she spoke coherently. It wasn't the usual vague sense of speech; the words came quite clearly, "Forgive me," she said, "I was curious." She smiled, a nice bright open smile. She was wearing a plain blue dress, and her eyes and hair were brown.

"It's a curious book," I said. "What is it a guide to, I wonder?" and I laid the book on the counter beside us. We looked at the following page together. It said, 'To Her Most Glorious Majesty'. I wondered which Majesty. "Queen Anne?" I suggested.

My companion said, "Or Elizabeth?"

"Not old enough," I said, quite certain about it, though there was no date on the book. I turned another page quickly. I was certain the dream would alter shape any second, or even just stop.

It was the Contents page. I read aloud "Of True Vision. Of the Nature of Visitation. Of Proper Commands." and then the book closed, quite of itself. I tried to open it, but I could not do so. It was as solid as if it were locked, and when I looked again I saw that it was indeed locked, with a clasp. "We need a key."

"Yes," she said, "but I don't think there is one. Perhaps we should ask the proprietor."

It was all so logical that I was staggered. We went to the back of the shop hand in hand. As we walked, the shop extended in front of us. The floor sloped upwards, too, and it became harder to walk. Before long the floor's slope had become so steep that we were leaning sharply forward, and then we were crawling, and we were no longer hand in hand.

"We'll never make it," I told her.

"But we will if we're meant to," she gasped, and she was quite right. The floor was suddenly level again and we stood up in front of a cashier's desk, behind which stood a young woman in green. She looked at us.

"No key?" She said, "No key," and then simply vanished. We looked at each other.

"It's like that in dreams," she said.

"You know it's a dream, then?"

"Of course," she smiled, "I'm dreaming you." She gave a little giggle. "All right, we're dreaming each other, but why the book-shop? Is that your dream or mine?"

"It could be mine. I like old books."

"So do I," she said, "I used to work in a library."

"Well, let's call it mutual. But what now? I mean, dreams usually shift gears around now, don't they?"

"I suppose so. But I like this place," she added, "I don't want to leave it—or have it leave us."

"I want to read more of the book," I told her.

"Don't think about it," she advised me, "whatever you do, don't think about it or it will vanish."

Her counsel came too late. The bookshop no longer surrounded us, and I was alone on the sea shore. I looked around for her. She was gone. I tried to envisage her face, tried very hard indeed, and, of course I woke up.

Now, I have often had coherent dreams, but this one was the most coherent I had ever experienced. I tried to go to sleep again, but was too aware that it was almost morning. The room was already brightening. I had to get up.

You'll not be surprised to hear that I thought about that woman and about the bookshop and the book most of the day, and especially about the young woman. It was perplexing. Could she really have dreamed me, or did I dream that she was dreaming me? I felt my mind becoming dizzy and confused. I was certain, though, that I would never see her again—but, following her advice, I determined not to think of her when I went to bed, not to concentrate on her consciously, just to drift off, not even hoping. I had to let the dream come to me. I knew I would never catch it if I chased it.

Well, they say dreams come in threes, and this would not be a story worth telling if I never saw her again, so you are correct in assuming that the dream returned to me. It did so that very night. Or rather, she returned to me, for the setting was no longer a bookshop, it was a graveyard, and dotted with huge tombs as well as the usual gravestones. We were sitting on a bench near a big mausoleum with a heavy wooden door. I turned to her and said, "Do you remember last night?"

"Of course I do. I keep a book by my bedside and I write down all my dreams."

"And then?"

"Then I get up, have breakfast, and go to work."

"Where?" I asked.

"At the College."

"Which College?" She looked puzzled.

"I don't know. I can't place it somehow. It's just a college. I'm in Counselling. What about you?" I thought for a moment.

"I don't know," I said, "or rather I know but I can't say it."

"Ah . . . it will probably come to you when I've dreamed you some more."

"Or when I've dreamed you."

We got up from the bench without saying anything else and walked towards the mausoleum. "It's a huge door," she said. "I wonder what it's like inside."

"Coffins I suppose," I suggested, "or sarcophogi. They must have been rich."

She pointed to some lettering carved on a big stone above the door, and spelled out, "Death is the only mystery we all solve."

"We must get in," I said suddenly. I pulled on the iron ring in the door. She joined her efforts to mine. Nothing moved.

We stood breathless and hot (I'd never felt hot in a dream before), and she said, "The woman in the gatehouse will have a key." I did not know how she knew there was a gatehouse, or that there was a woman in it, but off we went, and as we went the graveyard grew larger and larger, and the gravestones bigger and more tightly packed together, so that we had to squeeze between them. At one point we could only go farther by climbing over a mausoleum almost as big as the one we had just left. She said, "Damn! I've laddered my stocking." I licked at a scrape on the ball of my hand. Eventually we got on the top of the monster and looked down. The ground was a long way below us, and there a woman was standing. It was not the same one as in the bookshop. This one was older and wore a brown cloak.

I called down, "Can we have the key to the mausoleum?" She affected not to hear me. I tried again. She still did not hear. Then we raised our voices in unison and she turned and looked up at us. Her voice seemed a whisper, but it carried to us quite distinctly. "No key," it said.

We sat down on the top of the mausoleum, and I had a presentiment. "We must hold hands." She put her hand out towards me, but it was too late. I was once again alone on the sea shore. I did not waste time looking for her or thinking of her. I simply willed myself to wake, for I wanted to write it all down as I was sure she was doing.

I woke up quite easily and got out of bed. As I unbuttoned my pyjamas I noticed a graze on my hand. I didn't know what to make of it. How could it have happened? I decided I must have scraped it against something the previous night and not noticed. I did not want to think otherwise. I felt a little scared. I even told myself that I must not dream that dream again, but then I thought about her and decided that a graze didn't amount to much. It was not as if I'd broken a leg. So that night I went to bed expecting the story to continue. It did not. It did not continue indeed for a whole week, by which time I had grown quite nervous. I liked the woman, you understand. I wasn't in love or anything like that. I simply enjoyed her company, as if she were my sister, or cousin, or something of that kind.

Anyway, on the seventh night the dream returned, and this time we were both standing among trees on a small hill. Below us a lane wound through the fields and there were two cottages perhaps fifty yards apart. Children were playing in front of one of the cottages. "This is more pleasant," I said. She nodded.

"But, you know," she said, "I've been thinking. Each time we've met only one other person."

"Two persons," I interjected.

"Well, perhaps two versions of a person, and each time she has frustrated us. You say you are dreaming me and I say I am dreaming you—but what if she is dreaming both of us?" I felt suddenly chilled.

"I don't like that at all. I mean, she could wake up. But let's ignore that problem for the moment. Have you a name?"

"Yes, of course I have, it's . . . I've lost it," she said. "What about you?" I couldn't remember my name either. "Tell you what," she said, "let's be frivolous—let's say we're Dick and Jane. Let her dream her way out of that! Not giving us names, indeed!"

"What about the name of your College, then?"

"Not a clue," she said. "What do you do, anyway?"

"I'm a school teacher."

"What school?" I shook my head. "All right," she giggled, "let's beat the rap again. I work at St. Trinians and you at, oh, Greyfriars. How are you, Dick?"

"Just fine, thank you, Jane," I said, and we beamed at one another, and then, a little selfconsciously, looked away down the hill. A couple of toddlers were playing in front of the right hand cottage.

"More people," said Jane, "perhaps we're their dream!" As we watched, the door of the cottage opened and a woman in a black dress emerged. She called the children into the house, and then came out herself and went along the lane to the other cottage, knocked on the door, and went in. "She's old this time," Jane said thoughtfully.

"I wonder what exactly . . . . Whatever we feel we must do, we mustn't do it."

Jane looked dubious. "It might wake her up," she speculated, "and then where would we be?"

"I've thought of something. Was your knee bruised, I mean really bruised, when you woke up last time?"

"Yes," she said, "I thought I must have knocked it or something."

"My hand was grazed, too. Do you realize what this means?" She frowned.

"I suppose it means that we can take some effects back with us," she said.

"Yes. So if we broke our legs, we'd wake up with broken legs."

"You're not suggesting that," she said.

"No, but have you a pin, a needle, even a nail file?" She took the brooch off her dress and gave it to me. "I'm going to scratch a circle on your arm," I said, "and one on my own."

"But why?"

"Well, when we wake up it will make us absolutely certain that we really were here. That it wasn't all a dream."

"But it is," she said, "we've agreed on that. Still, what's a scratch among friends?"

I got the brooch and she winced a little as I did it. I suppose I winced myself. "That can't have happened accidently," I said. "When we wake up we won't try to believe we did it accidently and didn't notice, and so we'll know we're real."

"But are we?" she said. "I mean, what's real? Is that cottage real, for example?" And then, as we looked at the cottage, we saw a little plume of smoke curl out of one of the windows, and then there was a flicker of red. "It's a fire!" shrieked Jane. "The kids!" and set off down the hill. I was only a second behind her, but I had realized what was happening.

"This is a trap," I gasped. "It's happening again!" She paid no attention but ran on.

We reached the cottage together and grabbed the door handle. "It's locked," moaned Jane. "The woman must have the key." I grabbed her.

"No key— don't you understand? No key. . ."

"But the kids . . ."

"All right, but let me do the talking."

We hurried to the other cottage and knocked on the door. The woman who opened it was very old. I took a deep breath. I said, "I think you should go to the children. Their house is burning down."

She gave me an odd look and said, "The door is locked and there isn't a key."

I attempted a smile. "I'm sure you'll dream up something. Goodbye," and I turned my back on her, and Jane did the same. We walked across the lane, hand in hand. We were not about to let go of each other. We resolutely did not look back at the cottage. After a few moments I said, "We would have been burned, perhaps even burned to death if we had got inside." She was shaking.

"Yes," she said, "but what now?"

"I don't know. We'll find out, I suppose."

We climbed back up the hill, and only when we had reached our starting point did we turn round. The cottages had vanished and where they had been there was nothing but grass. "It's near waking time, I think," I said. "I usually end up on the sea shore, what about you?"

"On the sea shore. I often dream about the sea." We stood smiling at each other. "I think we part here," she said, "to different shores I suppose."

"Why not the same one?"

She murmured, "Who knows?" and gently took her hand out of mine.

I didn't find myself on the sea shore. I found myself in bed. The circular scratch was still on my arm.

I tried to find her, of course, but there are a lot of colleges in Canada and I didn't know her name. I tried a Personal in the *Globe and Mail*, asking Jane to contact the Dick of her dream, but got no results. It occurred to me that her college might not be Canadian at all. So I simply let it drop. I wouldn't be telling you this story, though, if nothing else had happened. It happened over a year later, actually. I was in my favourite bookshop on Yonge street when a woman came into the shop. Somehow she seemed faintly familiar, but I couldn't place her at first, and then—it must have been a trick of the light—or the way she turned her head—it came back to me, and I listened for her voice as she asked about a book. It was hard to tell, but there was something about the accent, and when she was asked if she had an account and she said, "No account," I got it. It was the long 'o' sound and the slight dwelling upon the sound of the 'c' that did it. I had to speak. I went up to her and said, "Excuse me, but I have a strong impression that we've met before."

She turned to face me. She was not quite any of the three women I had seen, being neither young nor old, and yet not exactly middle aged, but she was certainly the woman. She said, quietly, "I don't think so."

"Perhaps I dreamed it," I said, and then she smiled a strange smile.

"No, you did not—I dreamed it—and I'm still dreaming it or perhaps you wouldn't be here."

I was without words for a moment and then I asked the question: "And the other one?" I could not, for some reason, say 'Jane.'

"It's a mystery, isn't it?" she said lightly, giving the bookseller the kind of glance that indicated I was out of my tree.

"And you have the key," I told her.

"No key," she said.

I think I ran out of the shop. I know I can only remember finding myself in the street with her words still in my ears. They still come back to me when I have my attacks. Sometimes I am Dick and sometimes Jane, but whoever I am, I am dreaming the other, and always the dream ends up with those words.

Susceptibility

My PROBLEM IS THAT I AM SUSCEPTIBLE, or perhaps, as Mrs. Woodbridge put it one evening in the shower (her husband is a sailor, poor lady), amenable. "You're so beautifully amenable, darling," she said. Later she said other, more flattering things, some of them a little incoherent, but I do not need to repeat them here. Being amenable, or susceptible, or maybe both, I rarely feel as if I am more than minimally in control of my own life. Indeed, I think I may be one of those that someone described either in Shakespeare or a silent movie as Playthings of Fate, but when I said this to Mavis Lockhart as we were having a nightcap at her place after the theatre, she simply told me that I was a delightful plaything and continued unbuttoning my shirt.

I don't want to give you the impression that I am promiscuous, although I may already have given it. I simply accept what opportunities come my way and, for some reason or other, Fate seems to favour me with more than the average number. There's that word "Fate" again. It keeps cropping up. Cindy Loffmeier used it, I remember. "I just can't feel guilty about this," she said, "it was fated." I saw no reason to feel guilty at all and "fated" sounded a little melodramatic. I told her so, and she giggled and said I was sweet and asked me to get her a cigarette. I don't really approve of smoking in bed, but I did as I was asked, and as I padded back to her I noticed a man's photograph on her dressing table.

More out of a wish to make conversation than anything else, I asked her, "Who's that?"

"Oh, it's an Ex," she said.

"I didn't know you'd been married."

She lay back on the pillows and drew on her cigarette. "I wasn't. I mean we weren't."

"But you lived together?" I queried, I don't know why. I don't usually cross-question my bed companions.

"Well, not really," she said. "We had an arrangement. He wasn't the usual kind of man. He was different." I skated over the implication that I myself was a usual kind of man, and that a good deal of experience must lie behind the judgement.

"In what way?"

"Well," she said, sitting up and leaning over to stub out her half-finished cigarette in the ashtray beside the bed, "he would come round every Sunday afternoon at about five o'clock and read me a story he'd written, and then we would have a little drink and go out to supper. He never stayed the night."

"But he did, er, you did . . . ?" I queried hesitantly.

"Oh, no," she said. "That's one of the things that made him so different. I couldn't understand it at first. I mean I'm really quite attractive," ("Extremely," I interposed), "and I made it quite clear I was willing. In fact I was more than willing, I was eager, but he wouldn't have any of it. "

"He was gay?"

"Oh, not at all. He was married and had four children."

"A faithful husband, then."

"He may have been for all I know. I certainly wanted to believe that. It would have been a little insulting otherwise."

"Then why did you go on?"

"It was the stories, I think. They were quite wonderful. He wrote in French."

"I didn't know you knew French."

"I don't. I didn't understand a word."

"But he explained them to you?"

"Never."

For some reason I was growing a bit irritated. "He must have talked to you about them or about something at least," I said. "He can't have spoken French all evening. What did you talk about?"

"Oh, everything," she said. "He had a lovely deep voice and a marvellous accent. I could listen to him for hours."

"Which you did."

"Yes."

"How long did this thing go on?"

"Oh, months."

"And all that time you didn't . . ."

"Well, I had other affairs, of course. He didn't mind; why should he? I used to tell him about them and we'd laugh." I felt a tiny surge of rage, as if she had told him about me and they had laughed together. I was beginning to think that Cindy was one of those opportunities I might have done well to miss. She must have sensed my feelings.

"Darling," she said, "don't let's talk about him if it makes you uncomfortable. After all, he's gone, and we're here," and she snuggled up to me to show just how here she was. I couldn't respond. I felt as if he was in the room watching, probably making notes—in French which I couldn't read either.

"His photograph's not gone," I said, "you kept it." She gave up on me and moved back to her own pillow.

"Yes," she said.

"But why?" I asked. "Are you still in love with him—stories and all?"

"I never was in love with him," she said. "I mean, not in that way. It's just that he was different." She scratched herself under her armpit thoughtfully, a gesture I detest. "I didn't understand at first, but after a while I think I knew."

"Knew what?" I asked. There were the beginnings of a cramp in my right leg. I rubbed it viciously. She pulled the sheet back up under her chin.

"He needed me. He needed someone to sit and listen to the stories, like listening to music. He was a sort of musician, and someone who could understand the words wouldn't do at all. I'm a good listener you know—or I was for him. He had a marvellous voice." I almost told her she was a good talker too, but I restrained myself. The back of my neck was itching. I wondered about fleas.

"Tell me more," I said, and, I think, through gritted teeth.

"If you won't be upset. I don't want to bore you." It was rather like a dentist saying he would stop if I wished, but really it would be better to go ahead and finish the job.

"Go on," I said.

She sat up in bed, took her nightdress from under the pillow and huddled herself into it, and rested her elbows on her knees. She picked up the half-smoked cigarette from the ashtray and lit it thoughtfully. I noticed that her lipstick was smeared and found myself automatically rubbing my mouth with the back of my hand.

"After three or four of these Sundays I thought it might be a good idea to study French—I hadn't understood by then, you see—so I got a *Teach Yourself French* book, but there didn't seem to be any connection between the words I read in the book and the words I heard, and all the grammar made my head spin, so I gave up. I left the book lying around one day and he found it. He didn't say anything. He just looked at me, as if he were disappointed, as if I'd somehow betrayed a trust. I said quickly, 'I've given it up.' 'I'm happy about that,' he said. He said 'appy' actually. It was rather sweet.

"I couldn't help being curious about the stories, though. Over supper once I asked him if he couldn't just give me a sort of hint. Were they love stories, or ghost stories, or adventure tales, or what? He looked at me with raised eyebrows—he had great eyebrows—and said, 'But you can 'ear it! I can see it in your lovely face.' He was very sensitive to appearances. I used to dress especially carefully for our meetings and he always noticed new clothes. He was right, of course. Sometimes they were fast and funny and I couldn't help giggling, and sometimes they were slow and sad and I found tears coming to my eyes. Once or twice they sounded wrong, sort of mixed up, and puzzled me. He'd stop for a second if that happened and scribble something on the typescript. I suppose he was making a revision. I didn't comment, but I knew that I had helped and it made me feel all warm inside."

She was staring out into the distance; I might as well have not been there. I said, "That's understandable," in a rather remote voice, just to remind her of my existence. Also, she seemed to be getting a bit sentimental and I can't stand sentimental women, especially when they go on about their long-lost loves. I sneaked a look at my watch. It was only midnight, a lot too early to go to sleep and I couldn't think of a way to leave. Or, by now, to stop her. Maybe the phone would ring. I willed the phone to ring.

"I was, as I say, a good listener, and after a while, even though I didn't understand French, I noticed that one particular name kept cropping up. In fact it seemed to be in all the stories. I didn't know how to spell it, of course, but I heard it more clearly; it was 'Cindy.' It was my own name. The stories were all about me! Or were they? He could simply have used my name, maybe because I listened to them, like a kind of dedication: 'For Cindy who heard me tell them,' or 'read them,' or something like that. I was going to be in a book. I can't tell you how excited I was!" She turned to me. "You must understand that," she said. "I was really excited. Wouldn't you have been?"

"Maybe," I said. "It depends what exactly the stories were about. You told him about all your affairs, didn't you? Maybe he was just writing you up, using you as copy." I wanted her to feel insecure. I wanted to do something about that fat complacency of hers. I don't mean that she was fat, she wasn't, but complacent people always look fat to me, sort of psychologically bloated.

"I thought of that," she said, "but it didn't really worry me. I thought it would be fun, actually. I mean I could show the book— in translation—to my grandchildren, if I had any, and let them read what a rip I'd been. It would amuse them. Not that I've really been a rip, mind you. I've just had a healthy and happy—on the whole happy—love-life, and what's wrong with that? I mean *you're* not complaining, are you? And I'm not a slut!"

"No," I said, but I wished I dared say "Yes."

"Anyway," she said, "one supper I taxed him with it, and he

laughed. He said that the stories weren't about me at all, but about a middle-aged woman who lived in Quebec and had two children, and that he had named her Cindy long before he had met me. 'But I think it was partly because your name was Cindy that I wanted to get to know you better,' he said. I was rather disappointed. But then he added, 'If I were to write about this Cindy,' and he touched my hand, 'it would have to be poetry.'"

She was staring away into space and smiling. I couldn't stand it any longer. I said, rather nastily, "He was a quick man with a compliment." She paid no attention.

"He meant it, you know," she said. "I could tell from his voice. I knew every twist and turn of his voice by then. So I thanked him and said if he did write a poem about me I would certainly have to learn French, and he laughed. I don't know whether he ever wrote the poem but he did publish the book not long after he went back east, and he sent me a copy. Do you want to see it?" and she half got out of bed.

"No," I said, "and, darling, I hate to do this to you, but I've just remembered that I have to be home to receive a call from England at six o'clock in the morning. I think I had better go."

"What a shame," she said, almost absently. "Still, we have had a fun evening, haven't we?"

"Yes," I said, picking up my shirt. "Now you just go to sleep. I'll let myself out." On my way I turned the photograph face down on the dressing table. I couldn't help myself. She didn't see me. She was all curled up in the bed, looking like a child and absolutely at peace. I didn't slam the door. That was one mark up to me at least. I may be susceptible and amenable, but nowadays I don't think I'm quite as susceptible as I was, and I'm much less amenable. When

Mrs. Woodbridge asked me round for supper last week I told her I couldn't make it. She keeps a photograph of her husband on the bedroom wall, and it's more than I can stand.

The Quick Brown Gox

I'M TAPE RECORDING THIS, not typing it. I have to do it this way if I'm to tell the story at all. I suppose I might try writing it out by hand, but my handwriting looks like an unknown dialect of arabic with cyrillic interruptions and my typist would never be able to read it. I sometimes can't read it myself. So you see I have to tape record it.

You don't see, do you? How could you? It was unreasonable of me to expect it. But the whole thing is unreasonable, meaning without reason. At least I can't find a reason. And I thought at one stage I was losing mine, if you see what I mean.

I'm not being very clear, I'm afraid. But I'm not used to doing it like this. In fact I'm not used to this machine either. I had to borrow it. I daresay I ought to rewind and scrub out what I've said already and start again, but I'm a bit insecure about how the thing works, so I'm going to just forge ahead. Forge—that's a good word in the context—forge—forgery. It was forgery of a kind, but a strange kind, I suppose. But I'm not getting any forrarder, am I?

All right then, here goes. If you hear a sort of glug it's me having a drink. I'm not too secure about the pause button either . . . .

Now, I write stories, as you know by now. And I do the things on a typewriter, as you'd expect. Or I used to do them on a typewriter. Nothing flashy. Just a rather old electric thing with a bell that tells me when I've got, or am getting, to the end of the line. I mention the bell because that was really part of the trouble. I'm a one finger typist, like a lot of writers I know, but after the first few words I don't have to look at the keys, I just bash ahead. I'm really quite fast. And pretty accurate. And when I'm on a roll, everything coming easy, I just bash ahead to the bell, return the carriage automatically, and carry on. I don't look at the stuff for whole paragraphs at a time, if it's going smoothly.

Anyway, that morning I started my usual routine at around nine. I began by typing a letter. I like to get letters out of the way first. Then I'm not nagged by guilt when I start on my fiction. Not that the letters aren't sometimes fiction too, in a way, which is another point I suppose. Or a sort of point. Well, this morning I was writing to my cousin Francis. He'd sent me some bulbs for the garden, god knows why. I hate gardening. I don't have green fingers at all. In fact I'd call them black. My wife says I have acid skin and that has something to do with it. But where was I? It's difficult to keep track when you're just talking like this.

Oh yes, well, I started off "Dear Francis," and then I didn't look at the keys again as I went on, "Thank you so much for the bulbs. They were a delightful surprise and I know just where to put them." (I couldn't resist saying that.) I paused just for a second, I remember, and stared into space. I had nothing to say to him, really. Still I had to write something. I glanced down at the keyboard, found the first letter or two and then bashed on as usual.

"Our daughter Joyce is doing fine at University. She is enjoying herself a great deal and we expect great things of her." (Francis's daughter is a high school drop-out and works in a drugstore.) "Our son is in great shape, too. He's into athletics and body building." I stopped there, stymied, and wondered if I'd written enough to give the notepaper the air of having been used adequately. So I read what I had written, but it wasn't—I mean it wasn't what I had written—or thought I had written at all. I told you I was a one finger typist, didn't I? And a fast one? Well, sometimes speed betrays me and I find I've typed not the Quick Brown Fox but the Quick Brown Gox—hitting one key to the right of the one I'd aimed at. Sometimes if I'm going really fast that phrase, hallowed by all typing students, comes out as rhw wivl npem gpc, but that's unusual. Usually it's only a few letters, but I sometimes surprise myself with new coinages like "cuxk" for luck. I'm not sure cuxk doesn't sound a bit better, actually, sort of more, well, chancy. Where was I?

Oh yes. I looked down and read what I—or the typewriter—had done, and it went "Dear Francis, Why bulbs you stupid prick? You know I hate gardening. Joyce screwed up at the University, and I do mean screwing. She'll turn up pregnant one of these days, we're certain. Joe watches TV sports the whole damn day and drinks so much beer he's like a barrel."

I gasped a bit at what I'd read. And then I giggled. I hadn't really understood yet, you see. I thought I'd just happened, by a trick of the mind, to write what I was actually thinking instead of what I intended. I did tell you that letters were fiction too, didn't I? Well, I pulled the paper out, of course, and began again. This time I watched what I was doing as I was doing it and everything went smoothly until right at the end when I didn't look at the keys or the paper and rattled, "All The Best, Yours, Ted," which came out as "Fuck you, chum, Drop Dead." I began to sweat a bit at that, and did the damn thing all over again, watching every key and every letter and I got it right. I wrote the address on the envelope in large print. People can read my print. I didn't want to lose control again and have the thing posted off to Omsk or Khatmandu or somewhere.

As you can imagine, I was a bit weary after all that. Still, I told myself that it was just one of those things. My subconscious had recognized my dislike of Francis and my frustration at having to lie to him, and had taken over. Subconsciouses do that—is that the right plural? It sounds funny, but never mind—I mean often in a story things will pop up without my thinking of them at all. Sometimes strange things, too. Like the time I was telling a story about a couple in the suburbs arguing over their martinis and a camel poked its head in the window. I had a hell of a time with that camel. It just wouldn't go away and I couldn't think of any reason for it to be there. Eventually I shifted the whole setting to Saudi Arabia, and the arguing couple turned into sheiks. My editor complimented me. He said I was broadening my range. Maybe I was. Or something was broadening it for me.

Something—I thought my subconscious—was broadening me again that morning, I reckoned. And as the camel had been a success I decided I'd just carry on with the story I was doing, and maybe something would turn up to enliven it. God knows it needed enlivening. It was one of those Canadian Content jobs, and I'd got a wise old Indian woman I'd stolen from Bill Kinsella visiting a Montreal I'd lifted from Mordecai Richler and encountering a drunk poet who was based on—but I'd better not tell you that. Anyway, it was dead boring. But I thought it might be saleable.

Well, I'd got to the encounter. The old Indian woman, Ermintrude Laughing Water, was leaning against a garbage can in a back street looking down at this poet who was drunk as a skunk and squatting at her feet telling her he was the greatest poet since Irving Layton. It was all very realistic and symbolic and for all I know it may have been post modernist as well. I'll have to ask Robert Kroetsch. I sat down, set my finger to the keys, and, well, it wasn't the camel again, it was worse than that. I wrote, or something wrote:

"Ermintrude Laughing Water looked down at the poet. She was not laughing now. Nor am I. In fact I'm bloody near weeping at all this shit I'm extruding for the gullible masses who think that the adjective Indian actually defines somebody and that poets are given to sitting in gutters and spouting verse at anybody who is fool enough to come by. It all goes to show that the human race thinks in stereotypes. Why don't we make the Indian woman put the poet in the garbage can and roll it down the hill while singing the Marseillaise? That should confuse them."

I made the mistake of looking at the paper at that point. I'm sorry about that. I would have liked to know what happened next. But all that happened was that I didn't know how to carry on, and went away and got myself a coffee.

When I got back to the typewriter I tried again and this time the story went on just as before the interruption. It wasn't any better, but it wasn't confusing. I was rattling away quite happily. Ermintrude had taken the poet in hand and led him to a nearby cafe, where they were neither of them popular, she because of her race and he because of his bohemian appearance. Two outcasts they were, of course, and the whole thing was going to get quite profound any minute. In fact I started a new paragraph with the words, "The poet put down his coffee cup and reached over the table to touch Ermintrude's brown wrist." I was going fast by then. It was moving splendidly. But, a paragraph later, when I looked, I discovered that it had not moved in the required direction. It continued:

"Ermintrude looked at him coldly, for she had a cold. She was the only old Indian woman in Montreal who has ever had a cold in any story yet written. This shows how original this story is. If the poet was dressed in a pin stripe suit and wore a flower in his button hole, it would be even more original. And if you want something absolutely and startlingly novel why don't we make him spill his coffee in his lap and turn into Donald Duck. Maybe she could turn into something too. Knowlton Nash, possibly. And she could say, 'And now the Journal,' and wave a little flag. After which Harold Town could come in riding a wooden horse. It's all a question of whose reality we are investigating."

I goggled at this farrago of nonsense. Then I tore it out of the typewriter and this time I didn't have a coffee. I had something stronger.

I didn't work any more that day. I was too shaken. Then my common sense got the better of me. This was simply one of those things. All I had to do was carry on as usual and cut out the weird digressions and it would be just fine. So I decided to do that the next day. But I couldn't, you know. It was like that damn camel. I just couldn't. So I shoved the stuff into the file, the rather fat file, labelled 'Work in Progress'—a bit optimistically—and settled down to something else.

The something else was a letter to the Canada Council about a manuscript they'd sent me for a report on its quality and publishability. They do this to me from time to time. Well, this one wasn't as bad as usual. I mean I didn't fall asleep or have to sit on my hands to stop myself scribbling all over it and correcting grammatical errors. So I began my report, "This manuscript has some excellent qualities." After a bit you get to rattle these things off pretty quickly. Maybe, like letters, it's also a sort of fiction. I don't have to tell you what happened. The Thing took over. Or something did. But it was different this time. It was on a different track. The first few sentences read:

"This manuscript has some excellent qualities. I will never forget that red headed whore in Vancouver, her long shiny boots, and her blood red nails, and how she . . ." I looked at the paper then and saw what I had done. This time I was upset. I mean, I'm not ashamed of it, you understand, or I wouldn't be telling you. I was young at the time, and well, every dog must have his day, isn't it, or something like that, but I hadn't even been thinking about her. I'd forgotten her, actually, 'til then, or I thought I had. But still, it wasn't on to talk about it. I mean it just wasn't on. So I started again, and this time I did it all very slowly. Almost letter by letter. And I got as far as "Occasional syntactical clumsiness" when my finger simply refused to obey me. I would aim at a 't' and get an 'm.' The letters aren't even close on the keyboard. I would type, or attempt to type, 'symbolism' and I would get 'orgasm.' I gritted my teeth, and went even slower, and if I concentrated really hard I could get some words right. But it was a battle, a real battle, and it was a losing one.

I remember one sentence ran: "The imagery is green knickers and occasionally a mole on her backside which succeeds in impressing the like a bit kinky reader." I tried another dodge; I reasoned that it was my right forefinger that was possessed. I was thinking of possession by then. Well, wouldn't you? So I tried using the next finger along, which made it even slower. But after a few words the same stuff came out, so I tried my left forefinger which meant that I mistyped what I wanted to write and only got what I didn't want to write correct, if you follow me. So we got, "could be accysed of pastuxhe and the mole on her bottom."

What can you do when you're in a fix like this? I felt madly that I should try typing with my big toes, but it didn't seem practical. Then I thought of putting a pencil between my teeth and doing it with that, but I kept shoving the pencil in between the keys and getting it stuck. Finally, I gave up. There was no use fighting the thing. So I had a stiff drink, sat down at the typewriter, and let the demon or whatever, have its—or his—or her—head. If it, or he, or she—has or had a head. I'm not too well up on demons.

I don't know what happened to change it or him or her, but once I'd given up the struggle, it—I think I'll stay with it—abandoned my lurid past—not that it has been particularly lurid, really, but there have been moments, as with everyone I suppose, including radio evangelists, or so we're told, though why on earth it is considered such a big deal to have sex when you're preaching what is supposed to be a gospel of love I never could understand, not that it's a gospel of love any more mind you, it's more like a gospel of guilt, but where was I—oh yes—letting it have its head.

Well, I did that, and for good measure—if that's the phrase I want, which it probably isn't—they so rarely are, you know. I mean the first time around it sounds just great to say "the metamorphosis was discombobulating," but on second thought, "it was a surprising change" sounds better, cleaner, as it were—as what were, come to think of it? And should it be which instead of what? I'm sorry . . . I can't help rambling. I'm really not used to tape recording like this, but I'm not myself today.

I wasn't myself then, certainly. I knew it too, so as I think I remember myself saying, for good measure I decided not to look at what I had written until I'd done at least half a dozen pages. I had to start with words of my own, though, and for some reason the words "The loss or desolation" came into my head, so I popped them down and let my finger do the talking, as you might put it. Well, it went very smoothly. I had an enormous sense of freedom, especially after I'd taken one quick glance and discovered that it had given up on my past. I just caught the name Valentinian, and as nobody of that name has ever been part of my quite honestly hardly scandalous past I felt comforted and on I, or rather my finger, typed.

As I pulled the sixth sheet out of the typewriter I felt quite refreshed and really curious. I didn't look straightaway. I was busy remembering how Coleridge wrote *Kubla Khan*, and that woman—what's her name?—who wrote entirely new pieces by Mozart at dictation. Maybe I had been taken over by someone like that. I rather hoped it was Hemingway. Just think of the sales of a new Hemingway novel, or even a short story. Well, it wasn't Hemingway, though it was certainly not me. The style looked familiar though, and a bit stiff to my eye. Sort of formal. It might be a great unwritten work by some giant of the past, I thought. Well, I was partly right. It *was* a great work, but not an unwritten one. I had typed out the first pages of Gibbon's *Decline and Fall* and what was even more unsettling were the three words at the bottom of the sixth page—"To Be Continued."

I didn't believe it really. I thought that the demon, or whoever, was teasing me. It couldn't be serious. So after a bit of pacing up and down and muttering I sat down, and did another page, and found it was all too true. Gibbon was continuing. I didn't like to investigate further, but I forced myself to do it. In my edition of Gibbon there are 3921 pages. At the rate of, let's say, ten pages a day, the job would take me more than a year.

I took the typewriter to the shop and said I wanted to trade it in for another one. The man said, "Didn't it work?" and started typing. The first words were, "Red headed and black booted she looked like." I stopped him rather brusquely. I didn't want to end up in the pages of the *National Enquirer*. I said I'd changed my mind. I took the thing home again and locked it in a cupboard. When my next cheque comes in I'll get another machine. In the meantime you can understand why I'm using this tape recorder, even if you can't understand anything else any more than I can.

Well, at least I've got it off my chest. I hope my typist is good at working from tape, and will get the punctuation and spelling right. I guess I'll find out. I got her to type out the Ermintrude Laughing Water thing as a curiosity, complete with those interruptions, and for some reason she thought it was original. I sent it to a magazine just in case her instincts were right, and after all what had I to lose? What is more, they accepted it. Well, I suppose it does look kind of avant garde—post modernist do you think?—and it has Canadian Content, so what more could they ask?

The cheque came today, and tomorrow I'm off to get a new typewriter. I'm a bit nervous though. I mean do you suppose the demon or whatever can switch machines? I never thought of that. Maybe it could switch even to a tape recorder if it had a mind to. But it hasn't, has it? I mean I haven't have I, well, said anything I shouldn't. I wish I knew how to use the rewind and playback stuff. Maybe I'll get the owner to do it for me before I send this to be typed. After all, demons are tricky things and I mustn't blue knickers let my big round breasts and one of those very slow smiles

that besides I'm not really into eroticism it would be so embarrassing is my voice changing it feels as if it could be the splendid relics
of two temples almost an octave lower or rather of two religions
exhibited a memorable example of the vicissitude of human and
divine things.

The Bargain

I LIKE TO TELL PEOPLE I'M A WEEKEND SAILOR, and this invariably causes them surprise, if not shock. I let them mumble "How fascinating" and ask, hesitantly, "what kind of er . . . boat?" the hesitance being due, I imagine, to a nervous feeling that my craft might be a yacht. Then I explode my tiny joke. "Not that kind of sailor," I say, "—a Garage Saler. Every Saturday, wet or fine, I go round the garage sales. You'd be surprised at what I find!"

Well, some of them are surprised, but some happily confess that they too are addicted, and the stories of Garage Salers are just as elaborately exaggerated as are the stories of other sailors, or even fishermen. Our city is absolutely crammed with Garage Sales every weekend—little ones where the family has bribed its children to get rid of long unused toys by offering them the proceeds—bigger ones organized by people who are moving house or leaving the Province—strange ones from people who have, all too obviously, had a business failure and must get rid of their stock of dolls' clothing, costume jewellery, and plastic souvenirs—the variety is almost endless. Some are not truly Garage, but Yard Sales, and these may include lawnmowers, motorcycles, and even boats. And the prices can be quite startling! I mean, who could possibly pass up the purchase of a new suit for five bucks, and I do mean *new*. One of my friends now has sixteen. Unfortunately he rarely wears suits. Of course, occasionally one is obliged to regard one's purchases through those rose-coloured spectacles that come with every bargain hunters' kit. "It needs a little alteration, of course," is one of the phrases one hears fairly constantly, and one excuse when a fellow saler looks askance at some purchase is the mendacious "I really got it for a friend of mine." Habitual salers recognize these remarks as being what they are, but their own backgrounds are so filled with purchases of unlikely objects with minimum utility, that they rarely care to pursue the matter. And, after all, in due course they too will have a garage sale, and these prizes whose lustre has worn dim may be unloaded on some other addict. 'One man's junk is another man's treasure,' is the motto of every one in the game.

I would not be telling you all of this if I were not aware that there are still a great many people who scorn garage sales, buy their suits at The Bay or even Straiths. (Did I tell you I got a new, well practically new new, Harris Tweed for six bucks last month? It only needs a little alteration.) And there are those people who still feel that well-used kitchenware may harbour strange poisons and baccili. I myself, however, and my fellow salers have no such qualms, and I know one fashionably dressed young woman at a rather splendid reception, who replied to the question as to where she discovered her new gown by saying happily, and loudly, "At a Garage Sale. It cost me nine bucks." Rather to my surprise, her questioner was envious rather than contemptuous. Sometimes, however, one does not say, "I got it at a Garage Sale," one says, "Oh, I picked it up for a song," which allows the person to believe that one haunts Sotheby's or Christie's auctions. Auction-goers are another breed entirely. I don't associate with auction-goers. Auctions are not so—how can I put it—serendipitous.

Serendipity is the goddess of Garage Sales. One should never actually think of one's peregrinations round the suburbs as "shopping," and one should never deliberately set out to find something. One must leave it all to Serendipity. After all, who, in their senses, would go shopping for a velvet smoking jacket, or for a batik blouse with a dragon on it, and only one small tear? And when I bought my 1920s cocktail-shaker I was actually on the wagon.

But I'm putting off telling you my tale, perhaps because it is a little unnerving still. It began one Saturday when I was saling and for once without George. I enjoy saling with George. He has an eye for oddities, and bargains, and appreciates such otherwise unloved items as a copy of 1930s *Old Morre's Almanac*, or a pith helmet. There is a certain appeal some objects exert; they call out for affection, and occasionally one feels, "If I don't buy it, who will? It mustn't surely be abandoned to the garbage man!"

Some sales as a whole have the same quality, especially late in the day when all but the most assiduous salers have given up the hunt; one feels the disappointment of the owners very sharply; sometimes, indeed, there is a sadness you could cut with a knife.

It was that sadness that got to me one Saturday when, George being out of town, I saled off on my own. I did all the advertised ones, and a number that weren't advertised but just sprang up, so it seemed, on a whim, and I was into what was to me strange territory, looking for 598 Forest Drive, a most aptly named road, for the forest was thick on either side and only occasionally penetrated by narrow driveways to houses hidden in the trees. I found 598—the number was lettered on a polished slice of cedar at the driveway entrance—and set off towards my goal. I felt curiously certain that something was going to turn up, that something was, as it were, waiting for me. About a quarter of a mile up the driveway, which was really more of a lane, I glimpsed a log-built cottage to my left. It couldn't be 598, for the driveway-lane continued, but it clearly had a Garage—or rather Yard—Sale going on. The track to the house might have been all right for a small car, but mine wasn't, so I parked and went on foot and there I was, facing as fine a collection of junk as I had seen in years.

When I say junk, I mean it. Everything looked old, battered. There were fry pans, cooking pots, old knives and forks—not silver, I assured myself rapidly—one must be on the lookout for silver. There was a chair with a badly mended leg and the basketwork seat torn. There was a group of old bottles that would have delighted a bottle collector, but I am not one of those. The woman seated in one of the rickety chairs smiled at my "Hello," though her smile was terribly sad. She was middle-aged, but dressed in the sort of faded blouse and long skirt that one associated with hippiedom. She could be, I thought, a sometime flower child. I looked desperately for something to buy, but there was nothing. There were no prices either, and I did not want to ask a price and then upset her by not buying. Sometimes I bargain a little—George is excellent at that—but this was no place to bargain.

I was going to say, "Sorry, I can't see anything I want today," when my eye caught a splendid stag's head leaning against a tree stump. I went over and examined it. It was in perfect condition, the hide glossy, the glass eyes bright, the horns sharply pointed, and it had a magnificent spread. It was mounted on a conventional wooden shield, and there was a small brass plate beneath it, but it was too tarnished for me to read the words. Around the beast's neck, totally inappropriately, was a length of ribbon and a rather ugly bell. Now, I can't say I've always wanted a trophy of this kind—I haven't—and heaven knows I'm not a sportsman and could never bear to shoot anything—but this magnificent beast attracted me. I stepped back from it. Where could I put it? Over the mantelpiece? No, I thought not. My wife would object. It really belonged in a den or rumpus room, but my house contains neither. Obviously it had to be in my study. I could take down the painting on the wall facing my desk, and put this up instead. My wife always wanted that painting for the living room, anyway. "How much is this?" I said, as casually as I could.

The owner said, "Whatever you wish," and I was in a quandary. Ten bucks seemed a good round sum.

I said, "If you really want to get rid of it, what about ten bucks?"

"Take it. It's yours," she said. So I took it, silly little bell and all.

I hung it in my study that afternoon and got my wife along to admire it, which she didn't. "What on earth possessed you?" she asked.

"I don't know. I guess it's because he's so magnificent. And it would fetch a lot if it were in an auction."

"You should put it in one then, maybe."

"After I've got tired of it, perhaps," I said, "or maybe in a Garage Sale of our own. We'll have to have one sometime." She brightened at that.

"Yes," she said, "there's a lot of junk we could get rid of." I didn't ask her what junk. I rather thought I knew the answer, and it would have included a good many of my other Saturday bargains.

Well, we left it at that, and the next day I sat behind my typewriter and admired it. I was writing a story about a couple who had left the city to live in the boonies, and it seemed appropriate to have a stag looking over my labours. The bell, however, irritated me. I had meant to take it off and had forgotten. So I cut the ribbon and put it in the odds-and-ends drawer of my desk, and settled down to work.

Now, I don't know how familiar you are with the business of writing, but maybe you write stories yourself, in which case you will understand that every now and then one pauses in mid-paragraph to hunt for a word, or even, more seriously, to wonder what the hell ought to happen next. At such times one lights a cigarette, sips at one's long cold coffee, and stares into the distance with unfocussed eyes. 'Waiting for inspiration,' I suppose you'd call it, or, perhaps, waiting for Dame Serendipity to do Her thing—She deserves capitals, for without Her hardly any books would ever get written, believe me. Anyway, I reached the point where my couple had finished their first breakfast in their log cabin and I didn't know what to have them do next. They were sitting silently over their coffee and saying nothing at all and doing less. So I unfocussed, and found myself staring at, or maybe through, the stag's head, and somehow or other the two glass eyes seemed to be staring back at me. I hadn't really noticed their colour before. They were not so much brown as a sort of brown-red, and they seemed almost to be moving—not much, just a little. I said aloud to myself, "You're getting tired," and I lit a cigarette, and then, through the smoke of the first puff, I saw—or fancied—that the huge nostrils were wrinkling. "Silly," I said, and got back to my story.

I finished the thing fairly quickly, and decided the stag had brought me good fortune. I got up stiffly from my desk and went over to it, and patted it on the muzzle. "Thank you, friend," I said. Then my eye caught the brass plate. "I really must clean that up for you," I told him, and went in search of the Brasso.

That brass plate was terribly tarnished, practically black in fact, and I had to work very hard to make any impression on it at all. Eventually, however, a few letters began to be noticeable, and the beginnings of a date. I found a capital T and, a little further on, a capital L and a figure 9. I really sweated over it, and eventually gave up. I told him, "I'll have another go tomorrow." I was talking to him quite naturally. Well, one does you know. Or maybe I should say I do. Writing is a lonely business. I sometimes even talk to my typewriter.

That night I had troubled dreams. They were all about the stag. I wasn't surprised. I often find the day's concerns replayed during the night. Still, I didn't much enjoy standing in the forest and seeing that stag coming in my direction. I was in a clearing and he was opposite me. He pawed the ground, too, and lowered his head as if he was going to charge. I yelled out loud in my dream, and also apparently in actuality too, for I felt a blow in my ribs and it wasn't the stag's antlers but my wife's elbow. "You're dreaming," she told me. I was grateful for that.

At breakfast I was still uneasy, though, and my mood was not lightened by the cat who brought in a dead bird and laid it under the kitchen table. "That cat," said my wife, "has to have a bell. The old one doesn't seem to be working at all." As soon as she said it I thought of the bell round the stag's neck.

"That stag was belled," I said.

My wife said, "You don't bell stags."

"Well, someone belled this one. Maybe it was a Christmas stag—one of Santa's reindeer—which do you think?"

"Not Prancer or Dancer," said my wife. "Isn't there one called Blitzen—as in donner und blitzen—he has a sort of thunder and lightning look about him." I couldn't remember the names too clearly, so we gave up on that one, and I went down to my study and started revising the previous day's story.

I'd got about halfway through when I looked up to help me decide whether there were two c's or only one in raccoon, and this time the eyes were brighter and redder than before—or so they seemed—and the nostrils appeared to be positively alive, and, well, just for a second it seemed that the head had moved down a little and the horns were about to point right at me. It was so vivid an impression that I moved back on my typing chair and it skittered into the wall behind me, and I said, "Hell," and when I looked again the stag was back to normal.

After that I decided that whether Blitzen—but I really couldn't call him that, it sounded insulting—whether this stag brought inspiration or not, it was a bit alarming. Still, I thought I'd get used to him, and I finished my revision and had another go at the brass plate. This time I got more letters clear. It read: "To . . . . L . . . . s S . . . . 19 . . ." I decided that another session with the Brasso would make all clear and after lunch I settled down to drafting a review article for *Books in Canada*. I had celebrated the completion of work on the short story by having a glass or two of wine—well, maybe about half a bottle—with my lunch and I found myself dozing off a little in front of the typewriter.

I honestly don't think I really did drop off to sleep. I can't be certain, but I don't think I did. I did, however, drift into a funny state of mind, almost dreamlike, and I found myself staring at the stag, and this time there was no doubt about it; it was staring back. Moreover the head was definitely lowered. I told myself, "Nonsense," but somehow I couldn't get back to full consciousness at all. I was in a kind of daze, and behind the head, where obviously there was really only wall, I saw a sort of shadow forming, a shadow of huge gleaming hairy shoulders, and below the head there was a broad chest and it led down to two firmly planted legs and hooves. I sat there absolutely transfixed. It was as in my dream, only more so, if I can put it like that. And this time I couldn't yell. I was in a panic. My throat was clenched tight and I was absolutely glued to my chair. There was a smell in the room too, a dark earthy sweaty smell and the beast's head was now definitely lowered and the hooves were pawing what was now equally definitely turf. Turf in my study? Yes, turf. No doubt about it. And the beast was snorting. I hung onto the desk with both hands. At least there was a desk between us, but not much good it would do if the beast charged, as it was certainly going to do. I could not move and the red eyes were fixed on mine—like a stoat's—is it?—hypnotizing a rabbit. I made a heroic effort of will, but I was too late; there was a terrible noise—I suppose you'd call it a bellow—and the beast was on me, and my chair fell over backwards and I cracked my head, and for a moment I may even have lost consciousness. It was only a moment though. I scrambled to my feet and gave a yell you could have heard blocks away. My wife came running.

"What is it?" she cried. "What's happened?" I gestured weakly at the head on the wall.

"It charged me," I gasped. "It charged me!"

She said, "You fell asleep, didn't you?"

"No, I didn't. It truly . . ." then I paused. I said weakly, "I must have."

"Wine at lunch is always a mistake," she said. I nodded.

I said, "I'll be all right now," and as soon as she had left I got the bell and the faded ribbon out of the drawer and I tied the bell back on, I don't know why, I just felt I had better. That stag had to be belled.

I still felt more than nervous, though. After all, the bell could only warn me; it couldn't stop the charge. Or could it? I looked more closely at the bell, and I saw that something was scratched on it. I didn't remove it from the ribbon, or the ribbon from the stag; I took the whole thing down and got the Brasso again. It took a long time, but finally I was able to read the letters. The brass plate said, "Tom's Last Stag 1904," and on the bell, in quite small but deeply bitten letters I read: "PS CIV 9." I found the Bible back of the cupboard in the sewing room. The ninth verse of Psalm 104 read: "Thou hast set a bound that they may not pass over; that they turn not again to cover the earth."

That's almost the end of the story. I had no bad dreams after that, and the stag's eyes seemed ordinarily brown. I thought at first of putting it in our Garage Sale, but it didn't seem right, somehow. So it's still there, and you can see it any time you wish. Those few visitors who I let into my study have admired it a good deal, especially George.

"Where did you find it?" he asked.

"Oh, a Garage Sale up Forest Drive way," I told him.

"And why the bell?" he asked.

"It arrived with it, and it seems to belong." George nodded. He understands these things.

A month or so later there was a Garage Sale announced for 604 Forest Drive and so George and I included it in our rounds. When we got to 598 I said, "It was up there I got the stag. Funny old place. A lot of old kitchen stuff. Probably still unsold."

"Rosemary wants an iron skillet," said George. "Let's drive up there, in case."

So we drove up the long driveway-cum-lane, but you've guessed it, I couldn't spot the track to the place at all. I thought I'd found it once, but it was no go. So we went right up to the end and the man outside 598 looked surprised.

"We heard there was a Garage Sale," George said, rather cleverly I thought.

"That was a few weeks ago," the man said, "and just about everything went."

"Not absolutely everything though," said George. He's always unwilling to accept defeat.

"No," said the man. "But what's left is really junk. I'll show you." And he took us into his garage. "Old photograph frames," he said, "and a few books." I looked through the photographs. There was one of a middle-aged man and woman outside a log cabin.

I said, "This looks familiar."

"I can't think why," he said. "That place was in the bush down towards the road a way, but it was rotting away when my dad got this property in the depression. All I remember of it is a wall or two left standing. I was a lad then, and this house was just being built."

"Ah," I said. "Who owned it, do you remember?" But he couldn't, or didn't, and I paid him fifty cents for the photograph frame, and even George was surprised at that, though he didn't tell me I was wasting my money. Garage Salers never do that. Wives do, though. But I still have the photograph and on the back it says, "Tom and Lily, Summer 1904, taken the week before Tom was killed." The stag still hangs on my wall, but my wife wants to put it in our next Garage Sale.

The Break

THE REALLY BIG BREAK WAS HIS DYING.
You can see that. I mean, alive and kicking he could only be in one place at a time, and you could bank on having arguments about what he said here and what he said there, and all the fuss and feathers about conflicting witnesses. Dead, he could be pretty well everywhere at once, in a manner of speaking. People dreamed about him, you see. Well, it was natural enough. He was a pretty strong personality, charismatic you might say. So there he was, cropping up in one place during a siesta, and in another place hundreds of miles away by nightfall, and, I guess, sometimes even at the same time. Dreams are handy too, in another way. If a chap says he was told something in a dream—or maybe he'd call it a vision—you can't really call him a liar. You either take his word for it or you don't, but you can't challenge him. Of course some of those dreams were a bit strange, and a good many were vivid enough for people to say that he actually appeared, that it was his ghost that came to them, or something like that. It was all kind of

exciting. People got together and talked about it, organized se-
ances and such. Some people even had the idea that if he hadn't
died the way he did, it would have been a good thing to have
polished him off, just to get the benefit. Some even said that was
really what happened.

Anyway, you know what had to happen next. People started
remembering things about him, going right back to his childhood.
The tales were often a bit hard to take. You couldn't track down
who first told them, for a start, and some of the ones about him as
a toddler were pretty cornball. I mean, it's hard to swallow all those
yarns about precocious infants doing magic, making things fly, and
so on. A bit better, maybe, than the old one about the infant
Hercules strangling snakes in his cradle, but not much. Still, the
stories went on being told. Some of the people were embarrassed
by them, especially the ones who'd actually known him when he
was alive.

The magic bit was one of the problems. He certainly did have
the touch as a young man. He was a bit of a conjurer and a bit of a
healer too. He could spot hysterics just like that, and knew how to
handle them. It was quite dramatic: touch of the fingers, a firm
word or two, and it was all over most times. He got out of hand
once in a while, mind you. You may remember his stampeding that
herd of pigs. The farmer wasn't pleased at all and took a lot of
calming down. Anyway, there it was, and once they'd dug him
under, the stories got bigger and bigger and after a bit there were
so many you couldn't help believing some of them, and if you
believed some of them, why not all? I believe a good many of them
myself, though I can't say I've ever had a dream about him, or even
met anyone who has. It all adds up, though. There has to be
something in it.

What bothers me is the way the thing is growing. There were only a dozen or so people round him at the end, but now there are scores of them, maybe hundreds, and he's not been dead long. They're pretty persuasive, too. Lots of young men, and women, go for it. Some places you can't go down the street without someone asking if you've been saved, whatever that means. And then there's the speechifying. Some bigwig in the movement writes a long letter to another one somewhere else, and this chap stands up in the market and spouts it all out. Often it leads to trouble. Things get thrown at them. But I must say they're tough. They don't seem to care if they're chucked into gaol for disturbing the peace or insulting the city authorities or whatever. Some of them will get themselves killed before they're through. Then I suppose people will start dreaming about *them*, and telling some more stories, and so it will go on.

I tell you, it's a kind of madness. It wouldn't be so bad if they had a bit of tact, but they keep on saying that nobody else's opinions are worth a penny, that anyone who thinks different is not only stupid but wicked as well. Arrogant is what they are. I've never come across such arrogance—well, not often, anyway. They're well organized, too, and getting better organized all the time. Before we know where we are they'll have got themselves so established there'll be no stopping them. It'll be like an army. Some of them are saying this already. Well, you know what the army's like. Step out of line and you've had it. It won't matter if you did whatever you did for good reasons, or even if you thought you were obeying orders. It will be the army that matters. The army has to run things. That's what the army is for. This year that lot is the enemy and next year it will be another lot. Discipline's the key word. Discipline means stopping people doing what they want to do, and teaching them to obey the officers. And the officers! Can't you imagine them? Today you paint this wall red, tomorrow white. There's no point to it but it keeps you from thinking about anything else or doing what they say you shouldn't. There'll be flags and banners, of course, with his picture on them, but nobody will be bothering much about him. What he said won't matter a horse's turd: it's what the army says he meant that will matter more than what he said when he was alive—or what we're told he said. And I can see this army taking over just about everything. Well, I won't be alive to see it, and when I'm dead I don't suppose anybody will dream about me. I certainly hope not.

They're all so gloomy, too. I can't understand it. They don't make bonfires to jump through and dance around like the rest of us. They don't have races and wine festivals and circuses. They sing a bit, but only about him or God or salvation. They're half of them scared out of their wits because if they put a foot wrong they won't be saved. There's that word again. I'm not sure but I think they mean being saved from horrible things happening to them when they're dead. You have to be miserable now in order not to be miserable later. I prefer those people who say that we come back again and have another shot at living, though I'm not sure I want to come back myself if this lot ever gets in charge. Well, I was brought up differently. "Live well," my father used to say, "and obey the law. Help your neighbours and they'll help you." I've done that mostly, I reckon. I'm not a religious man, but I have the good manners to go to the right temples on the right days, and I leave out stuff for the household gods. It's not that I believe in them completely, but it's kind of pleasing to make gestures like that, makes you feel good in yourself. It's a sort of thank you for being alive. And when times are bad, well, why not have a bit of trust that things will come right if you do your work and give to the temple? I mean, there's something in it, there has to be, though nobody can be sure just what it is.

But these people *are* sure. That's maybe the trouble. They daren't think they might be even a little bit wrong or they'd be in trouble, not just with the high-ups, but with their God. And there's only this one God, too. Apart from him, of course. They can't go on like this. They'll have to get a few more, if only little ones. At least I know which temple to go to when I'm sick, or when the money runs out, or even if a love affair goes badly—though I'm past all that now. I can see them making up a few more stories sooner or later. There are one or two already. One chap who was a netmaker died, so if you're a fisherman you ask him to protect your nets. Well, that's harmless enough. But this other stuff is nasty. I mean saying that everyone else's gods are false or evil and so on. Some of them even think that these false gods are a sort of enemy that wants to destroy us. I can't see it, myself, but then I was brought up differently. Each to his own beliefs, I say. I wish everyone thought like that.

Wishing doesn't get you anywhere, though. I've wished for a lot of things in my time, and not too many have turned up. Maybe I should have given more to the temples. My wife used to tell me that, and maybe there's something in it. But not too much, you know. What good does it do anybody if you give everything away to the temple or even to the poor, as these people sometimes say. He was all for giving everything away to the poor. I can't see it myself. You end up being poor yourself and looking for someone to give stuff to you. It might make some people feel good, but I wouldn't feel good about it. You have to have a little pride in yourself, a little independence. Some of them don't think like that at all; they're always begging for this or that—well, not even begging, some of them; they think it's their right to take stuff from people just because they spend their lives persuading people to believe in him. They'll get that organized into a system in time, you can bet on it. Everyone will have to give to them. And then their generals will get flashy uniforms and big houses to show how important they are, just like they always do. And the poor will still be poor and they'll go along with it all because they can't do anything else.

You can tell me I'm prejudiced. Maybe I am. It might not get to be as bad as all that. I mean, some of them are good people—sincere and kind—and they do look after one another. And he seems to have been a sweet man, and perhaps even something of a genius. He said some good things, though I don't really understand everything he said, or is supposed to have said. And he did help a lot of troubled people. It's a pity he died so young. If he'd lasted to be old, or at least not died the way he did, there might not have been so many wild stories, and things might not have got so out of hand. He could have settled somewhere with his little group of followers and nobody would have bothered him. And when he'd gone, his followers could have stayed on in whatever village they had, and enjoyed the teachings he left them, and not gone out rampaging all over the place getting people to change their ways.

They were mostly young, those followers, or you could say in the prime of life, and something gets into men around that time. Into some men, anyway. They have to be a success, make their mark on the world, stir things up. I'm not sure that stirring things up ever does much good in the end. "Slow and steady does it," my father used to say. They're fast moving and impatient. They want to take over the world—yes, the whole world. They may even be successful. It's funny, really. He once said something about not wanting to rule the world. If he'd lived a bit longer they might have seen the point. Or maybe they'd have left him and moved on to something or someone else, for all his charisma. But they made him a Cause.

I'm sorry for people with Causes. They never have time to think of anything else. I don't think I've ever had a Cause, and maybe I don't know what it feels like. I guess he himself had a Cause though. And it killed him. But he lives on, they say. He's inescapable. Well, I've managed to escape him so far, anyway, though they keep coming round to the door with their speeches and smiles. I suppose, being young and full of energy with nowhere to go, they did deserve some sort of break. But I'm sorry the break was his dying.

The Bingham House

I DON'T EXPECT YOU TO BELIEVE THIS. I'm not entirely sure that I believe it myself. But it happened, I swear it happened. And for all I know it's still happening, though I don't live there any more.

But I've begun at the end, haven't I? I'm always doing that, my wife says. She says one of these days I'll start the meal with baked Alaska and finish up with the soup. I don't see why not, actually. What's wrong with reversing things sometimes; it sort of freshens life up. And doesn't everybody look at the Classified pages before the headlines at least once in a while?

Actually that's how it all started. We were house-hunting, my wife and I, and we did look at the Classified section first, and there it was: 'House of Character for Rent,' and the usual list of rms, bdrms, receps, and so forth. We rang up the number given and went around and fell for the place straight away. It was one of those old houses built before the turn of the century by a sea captain or at least someone connected with the sea. There was a tower on it with one of those little balconies—Widow's Walks do they call them?—from which one could see the harbour. The windows on the top floor were like portholes too, and there was a lot of brass about the place and a general cabin quality about some of the rooms.

The bedroom had built-in lockers like sea chests, and there were several barometers actually screwed into the wood panelling. The turret room had a big lamp in it, as if it were a lighthouse. It was all very charming, and I was surprised that the various owners it must have had since the 1880s had left it relatively unchanged. Of course there were some alterations. There weren't any fridges in the eighties and the kitchen had a huge one, and the plumbing looked modern. The furniture was a mixture of old and new. Some of it was definitely antique, but not so much so that it would have excited any really perceptive dealer. It was just solid old stuff, and some of the pictures were old as well. I asked the agent who had been living in the house before us recently, and he told us that it had been in the same family since it was built and was generally known as the Bingham House. He seemed to feel this proved something or other.

"The family died out?" I hazarded.

"Oh, no," he said, "but the present owner is a widower and elderly, and he has moved to a condominium."

"Why hasn't he sold it?" I asked.

"He just won't," said the agent. "He says he wants to hand it down again, but as I understand it the only one of his immediate family left is a young man in Europe, a student, I don't know where."

"So he'll come back and claim his inheritance. How long will it be before he gets his degree?" The house agent shrugged.

"Can't tell," he said, "but you can have a long lease if you like —and if you agree to the conditions."

"How long, and what conditions?"

"Would five years suit you? . . . if you want to give it up before then you could give three months notice without penalty."

That seemed too good to be true, especially as the rent was low, but I was cautious. "And the conditions?"

"Not many," the agent said. "It's a family house, as I told you, and the old man doesn't want anything to be changed too much. The barometers have to stay put, for example, and you mustn't redecorate the dining room. That was the heart of the house in the old days," he said, showing the kind of sentiment one does not expect of house agents. "I mean, that was really where they lived. The present living room was the front parlour—for Sundays and visitors only," he said with a grin. "It's already been altered a bit—the furnishings anyway. But the dining room is much as it always has been. Who would want to throw out that big refectory table—good oak—and those chairs anyway? And the desk is a masterpiece of Victoriana."

I looked round the dining room and had to agree. It was still very much of its period, and there was nothing much I would want to change. It was rather dark, though, in spite of the sizeable window looking out to the front of the house, and the two porthole windows on the other outer wall were too small to give much additional illumination. Moreover all the walls but one were panelled in dark pine, and the exception was papered in a particularly ugly fashion—big red flowers on a ground that might once have been off-white, but was now a stale cream. The impression wasn't helped by the presence of a big marine painting in a heavy gilt frame. "Not even that wall?" I asked.

"No," he said firmly. "And the picture has to stay."

I stared at it. "It's the kitchen behind that wall, isn't it? I can't understand why there isn't a serving hatch."

"Yes," he said. "I know it's a bit awkward to have to go into the hall to get into the kitchen, but the two doors are close together, so it could be worse."

"I suppose so," I said, "but that painting is, well, not really my style." The agent looked at it judiciously.

"You could make it a feature, hang another couple of marine paintings on either side of it, or something. It would help hide the wallpaper."

I turned to my wife. "What do *you* think?"

"It's not that bad," she said, "and it *is* unusual." 'Unusual' is a term of qualified approval in my wife's vocabulary. "And the rest of the house is fine," she said. So we took the place. Why not? As my wife said, a couple of standard lamps would brighten the dining room no end, and we could hang some more pictures on the panelling, surely. There wasn't any law against that, was there?

"Oh no," said the agent, relaxing a little, "you can hang anything you like as long as you don't make too many holes, and leave that big picture where it is. I guess it's a family heirloom. Maybe the ship belonged to the family."

"Well, it's being wrecked now," I said. "Quite an effective storm at sea, I'd say, wouldn't you? Any more places we can't redecorate?"

"Not really," said the agent. "There are a couple of pieces of furniture he doesn't want dumped in the basement, and the fixtures of course. But you wouldn't want to move them anyway."

"No," I said, "I don't imagine so. So the rule is, if it's nailed on, or fixed, we don't unfix it?"

"That's right." He looked at the oil painting. "It's a great period piece," he said with enthusiasm, and it was with enthusiasm that we moved in a month later.

It was a good house for us, big and roomy, with plenty of scope for the kids, who adored the turret room, and thought the porthole windows were terrific. 'Neat,' they said. It was the year that 'neat' was the word to use. It wasn't long before we hardly noticed the painting in the dining room, and we had lightened its impact a bit with a couple of more modern pictures less gloomy in tone—good big watercolours of shorescapes, calm pictures. My wife called them The Calms, and the middle one The Storm. "Together they make a sort of message," she said, "before and after a storm there is always calm."

"It covers up that bloody awful wallpaper," I said.

Anyway, things proceeded quite normally in that house, if any household that contains two schoolboys can be said to proceed normally. There were no creaks and groans and no funny smell; there were no odd noises. It was all wholly commonplace. That made it all the more of a shock when one night just as we were going to bed we heard an almighty crash and dashed to the kids' room only to find them both happily and, I fear, grubbily asleep. "The noise wasn't from here, anyway," I said. And my wife said, "No, but it's the first thing one does, isn't it! I think it came from downstairs." So down we went and there in the dining room we saw the cause. The huge oil painting had fallen down. The string, or wire, or whatever, must have parted. Mercifully, as it was an oil, there was no glass to break, so we said, "Oh ah," and went back to bed, intending to deal with it in the morning.

Actually, I had to go off to work and so my wife was left to get some picture wire and rehang the thing. When I got home that evening, though, the picture was still not in place. I said, "You didn't hang the picture."

"No," she said. "I thought you ought to take a look first."

"At what?"

"At what was behind it." She pointed. When the picture had fallen some protruding wire or something had torn a great gash in the wallpaper.

I said, "It doesn't matter. The picture will hide it."

"Look closer." And I did, and where the paper had been torn I saw a gleam of something like glass. I pulled a bit more paper away and sure enough it was glass. "It's a window," said my wife, "into the kitchen. The other side is covered by that cupboard thing that's screwed to the wall."

"So what?" I said. "We just ignore it."

"I don't know so much," said my wife. "I thing we ought to uncover it."

"It's against the agreement," I said.

"To hell with the agreement. They're not going to throw us out for uncovering something that's really part of the original house. And we can hang the picture somewhere else in the room, after all. In any case," she added, "who's to know? The owner never comes round, and the agent doesn't give a damn, and if either of them asked to visit we could hang the thing back in moments."

When women are logical there's no way of gainsaying them, so we got a Stanley knife and did a bit of cutting, and the paper peeled away surprisingly easily and after a while there it was, another and quite sizeable porthole, complete with brass rim and fittings, and obviously intended originally to act as a serving hatch. Of course it was no use to us as it was, because the other side was blocked by the wall cupboard. That didn't deter my wife. "Let's take the cupboard down," she said, "then we can use this. It's made to open like a door and it will really be useful. It will be so much better than having to carry things out into the hall and in again."

"Yes," I said dubiously, "but . . . "

"Don't be a worry-wart," she snapped—she does snap sometimes—"we can get that cupboard down easily enough; there are only a dozen screws. And we can put it up again quick if we have to. Surely the spirit of the agreement matters more than the letter. We aren't really altering. We're not taking anything away." So I agreed.

I must say that it was a great success. We polished the porthole's brass and cleaned the glass that very evening, and the next day we had breakfast in the dining room instead of the kitchen and my wife passed the dishes through the porthole, and the two boys thought it was 'neat.' They even tidied up afterwards, because they enjoyed passing the dirty plates back through the porthole. The whole operation was a great success, and for some reason my wife looked positively complacent when I left her to drop the boys off at school and go on to work.

When I got home around five my wife met me on the doorstep. "I'm glad you're here," she said. "I've something to tell you."

"The boys?"

"Oh, no. I picked them up from school and they're playing in the turret. It's the dining room."

"What about it?"

"Well," she said, "when you'd gone I switched off the lights in there, finished tidying up, shut the porthole and went back into the kitchen. I was doing the usual things and thinking of nothing in particular. I had the radio on as a matter of fact, when I turned around and happened to glance through the porthole. Well, it is darkish in there with the lights off, and that glass is a bit thick as you know, so I couldn't be sure really that I saw very much, but I did see something—a figure—I mean a man—like a shadow really—and he was sitting at the far end of the big table. It gave me a shock, I can tell you. I went closer to the porthole and looked harder, and as I looked, it—he—lifted his head and, well, it was the oddest thing, I felt like an intruder, and I turned away. I wasn't frightened, you know. I wasn't a bit frightened, but . . . it was disturbing.

"I couldn't go on with what I was doing after that—not easily anyway—and—you'll think I'm stupid—but I got one of those bullfight posters we picked up in Spain the other year and I cello-taped it over the porthole. I still felt a bit nervous, though, so I rang Moira and we had lunch and did some shopping and I picked up the kids after school and took them to the Dairy Queen. It will be take-out Chinese tonight. I haven't been in the kitchen yet—or the dining room."

She was shaking a bit, so I put my arms round her. "It's not that I'm scared," she said, "not really, just unnerved. It isn't quite the same. It's a sort of not knowing, but feeling everything has altered."

"Yes," I said. "Let's investigate together. First, I think, the dining room."

Well, we went into the dining room and there was nothing untoward there at all. The Storm was still on the floor. "We ought to hang it up again," I said, "over the porthole."

"I'm not so sure," she said. "I think maybe if we just blocked the porthole we'd always be wondering. We could hang it to one side and put The Calms above each other, couldn't we?"

"I suppose so," I said. "Anyway, we should rewire it. Did you get any wire on your shopping expedition?"

"Yes," she said, rather proud of remembering. "It's on the chest in the hall."

"Go get it," I said, and turned the picture round. There was a piece of paper, rather yellow and dusty and cobwebbed on the back, but the writing was still clear—a real copperplate it was. It read "The Wreck of the Mary Deare," and underneath, "The Mary Deare was lost at sea off the West Coast on October 13, 1886. The captain and ship's company was saved. This picture was painted by Jacques Bouvier, R.A., in memory of the event, and placed in the Bingham Residence by Francis Bingham, captain and owner."

My wife came back with the wire, and I showed her what I'd found.

"Perhaps it was Francis Bingham I saw," she said.

"Maybe," I said. "Maybe." And we rewired the picture, though we didn't hang it again. We thought we'd decide about that later, and I turned off the lights and we went into the kitchen and she put the kettle on for tea, while I looked through the leaflet from the Chinese take-out place, but I caught her glancing from time to time at the bullfight poster, and I know I did so myself.

We sat at the kitchen table and had tea, and then, quite suddenly, she got up, went over to the poster, drew a deep breath and took it down. I went and stood beside her. "You see," she said, and I saw. It wasn't just an hallucination of hers, as I'd feared. It, or rather he, was there all right—but he wasn't sitting at the table; he was walking up and down. I couldn't make him out too distinctly, but he appeared to have a beard and a peaked cap and was wearing dark clothes. "You see," she whispered again.

"Yes," I said, and then, as we watched, another figure came into view, a woman. She went to the man, and seemed to be speaking to him. She was more shadowy than he. I got an impression of a longish neck and piled up hair and full skirts—I couldn't tell colours—it was all a bit misty. Automatically I rubbed the glass with my sleeve, but it made no difference.

"Ghosts," whispered my wife unnecessarily.

"Yes," I said. We watched, fascinated, expecting them to fade as ghosts are surely supposed to do, but they didn't fade at all. I took a deep breath. "I'm going in there. Keep watching."

Well, I must admit I was sweating. I wasn't frightened really, but excited, anticipatory. I went out into the hall, faced the door of the dining room, put my hand on the knob, turned, and went in. There was nobody there. I walked around a bit, but everything was normal. I went to the porthole and opened it, and "Well?" I said.

"They vanished," she told me, "just as soon as the door opened. They just went—as if they'd been switched off—as if you'd broken the circuit or something."

I went back to the kitchen, leaving the porthole open, and we looked in again, but there was nothing to be seen. "You've sent them away," my wife said, almost accusingly.

"Maybe I have, maybe I haven't," I said. "Anyway, let's order the Chinese food, and tell the boys to wash up."

Everything was normal after that, and it wasn't until the boys had gone to bed, and we'd had our usual evening watching television in the living room that anything else occurred. My wife had left we watching the Journal and gone into the kitchen to make our supper drinks, and I was just settling down to some interview or other when she came back. "They're there again," she said. "I just closed the porthole and as soon as I closed it, there they were. I guess I completed the circuit or something." I went with her, of course, and sure enough they were there again.

"Open the porthole," I said, and she did so and they were gone. "It *is* a circuit," I said. "It must be. Let's try something else. I'll just go in there for a minute and leave the door open when I come out." So I did that and then we closed the porthole and nothing happened. "Keep watching," I said, and went out and shut the door.

She called immediately from the kitchen, "They're back!"

We'd almost got used to them by that time and we stood and watched them for quite a while. Eventually my wife said, "I'm tired. Let's go to bed," and then, after a pause, "Open the porthole first. I don't want to think of them talking underneath us all night, and besides, the boys may be first in the kitchen in the morning." I didn't point out that it was a school day and that therefore they would certainly stay in bed as long as possible; I just did as she said and off we went to bed.

I admit that we neither of us slept too well. In fact, after a while she said, "Are you awake?" And I was, and she said, "Why ghosts? I mean, did something dreadful happen? Murder or something? And the owner must know about it, because that's why we hadn't to take the picture down and find the porthole."

"Yes, but they were just talking."

"I wish we could tell what they were saying," she said, "but the glass is too thick—you can't hear through it—and if we open it up even a crack . . . "

"Maybe we could try a listening device. Maybe we could bug the room." She giggled at that.

"I never heard of bugging ghosts. Do you think it would work?"

The oddest thing about the whole experience is that we began to treat it so matter of factly so quickly. It had become just a problem to be solved, and we really weren't alarmed at all. "I'll get a bug from somewhere," I said. "They have those intercom things for babysitters don't they? Maybe that would do the job."

"Well, I'll tell you one thing. That porthole's staying open all day tomorrow, and we're having breakfast in the kitchen." We weren't frightened, as I told you, but we were a little nervous. "It's the kids," she said. "Kids pick up things, you know—they're more sensitive." I wasn't too sure that our kids were particularly sensitive; they struck me as being quite ordinary schoolboys, and particularly insensitive to subtlety of any kind, but I could be wrong. Kids are odd creatures.

Anyway, I got one of the babysitting things and fixed it up, and took the wire under the door from the dining room into the kitchen, and that night after the kids had gone upstairs we shut the porthole and there they were again.

"Switch it on," my wife whispered, so I switched it on, and, sure enough, there were noises. They weren't intelligible noises, though—just rustlings and static. "It's the machine," said my wife, "it needs an aerial or something."

Well, I know even less than she does about such things, and I was dubious about that and couldn't work out how to fix an aerial in any case, so we just watched them, and the static and the rustling went on until the man lifted his hand and brought it down on the table with a thump, and we heard the thump. But only just. "Couldn't we ask them to speak up?" said my wife. "Put a notice in there: 'Speak Louder, we're deaf!' "

I said I thought not. "They probably don't know we're here. I mean, surely they don't know they're dead even."

"Maybe not," she said.

"Ghosts don't know they're ghosts; if they did they wouldn't be," I told her firmly enough to hide my lack of conviction.

"Well, the intercom's a bust. Maybe we should learn to lip-read. But I can't see their mouths clearly enough, can you?"

"No," I said, and we just sat and watched them. It was better than the TV.

"Like a silent movie really," my wife said. "Maybe we should get a piano." One does get frivolous at times of tension.

I needn't tell you about the next week or two. There's not much to tell. After ten days or so we paid them no more than a cursory attention. We looked in on them, you might say, from time to time each evening. Sometimes he was alone, sometimes they were together walking and talking or just sitting. There was no tension in any of it, which made it all the more surprising when the thing happened.

It was around the second week in October and for several days we'd not seen him at all, only her, and sometimes the room had been empty. When she was there she was usually wandering about, with something in her hand that looked even more shadowy than the rest of her. My wife spotted what it was first of all. "It's a duster," she exclaimed, "she's dusting." And that seemed to be the explanation. In point of fact we were getting a bit bored with the situation. I do feel that the least the household ghost can do is provide a little entertainment.

It was latish one evening that my wife came running into the living room. "Something's happening," she said. "Something's happening!" I ran back with her and we bumped heads as we reached the porthole together. The woman was still alone, but she was pacing up and down and holding something in her hands. "A letter," said my wife, "or a message of some kind."

The message or whatever it was obviously distressed her, and it was her distress that had roused my wife to call me. As we watched she crumpled up the piece of paper and threw it right across the room and lifted her shadowy hands up to her high-piled hair and pulled, and the hair came down and she bent over in what seemed to be pain. "Switch it on," said my wife urgently, so I switched on the intercom—we hadn't been using it for a long time—and the static was louder than ever before—really crackling and hissing. "She's upset," my wife whispered. "Bad news," and then "Ohhh," for the old man had suddenly appeared in the room.

The woman turned to him, and the static was increased to a storm of hisses and crackles as she put both her shadowy hands to her heart and fell forward into his arms. We watched, breathless. He held her up for a moment and then carried her over to a chair, and knelt in front of her. He seemed to be holding her wrist. And then he bent his head and laid it in her lap, and the intercom gave a sort of screech and went dead. My wife's hand was in mine, and she was whimpering. I had a lump in my throat too. "It's the shock," my wife sobbed, "it's the shock that's done it. He should have warned her." I said nothing. I was baffled. "Leave them," said my wife. "We can do nothing."

"I'll open the porthole," I said.

"No, it would be unkind." I did not understand her, but I switched off the kitchen light and we did not stay to make our supper drink, but went up to bed.

We lay awake that night too. "You see what happened," my wife said. "She did not know he had been saved, and he just turned up. It was the shock!"

"Saved?" I said. I was bemused.

"The wreck," she said. "The Mary Deare. It must have been her name too."

"That's a bit of a leap, isn't it?"

"No. Don't you know the date?"

"October something," I said.

"October the sixteenth," she said. "The Mary Deare was wrecked three days ago, and she got the news, just before he came back. It was the joy that killed her, it was the shock. And ever since, they've been here remembering their years together, and talking and, well, just living on, being at home together, until once in every year it all comes back."

"Ah," I said. "Yes, and the picture is the wreck of more than a ship."

"Yes," she said.

Well, that's almost the end of the story. We closed the porthole and hung the picture back over it. "It seems more decent," my wife said. "Let them enjoy their times together without our intrusion." But the following October we took down the picture and the wall cupboard on the other side and left the porthole open for a full month. "We can at least spare them that," my wife said, and every October after that we did the same thing. We stayed in that house much longer than five years. In fact, we stayed ten, and only moved out when the owner died and his grandson decided to sell. We would have bought it, but the price was too high. We did get it listed as a heritage building, though, so that nothing could be altered, and for all I know Francis and Mary Bingham are still there in the dining room talking over the old days, but we worry a little still every October.

The Activists

IT BEGAN WITH MAUD BATHURST'S
little boy. She had given him fifty cents or so and sent him out of
the house, as she was having her Woman's Group meeting that
morning, and when it was all over, the coffee drunk, the granola
cookies transformed into crumbs, and the reports read, he wandered into the room with a bag of jelly babies. He was only eight
and could not really be blamed for his intrusion, though older and
wiser folk, myself included, wouldn't have gone in there with an
armed guard. Anyway, Joyce Tregeseal gave a sudden cry of shock
and horror, and pointing at the child with a trembling finger,
hissed "Babies! And he's biting off their heads!"

Now all the world, except possibly Joyce Tregeseal, knows that
the only proper way to begin to eat a jelly baby is to bite off its
head. To Joyce, however, the act was symbolic of the masculine
attitude towards women and child-bearing and had something to
do with human sacrifice and abortion. Indeed, she made this very
clear. "Abortion!" she wailed, "the destruction of Life!" The other

women gazed at her in some astonishment at first but rapidly got the picture. Maud grabbed the bag from the boy. "Never buy these things again," she said. "They should never be allowed on the market!" He looked at her with as much astonishment as grief.

"Why, Mom?" he enquired, with more courage than I would have given him credit for.

"Because they're . . . er . . . nasty," said Maud almost firmly.

"They're good," asserted the bold child, "especially the black ones!"

A collective wail went up from the group, or so I was told later, and Hedda Skopf said in ringing tones, "We should boycott the store!" And that was how it all began.

I do not suppose you heard of the Great Jelly Baby Boycott of Centreville. It got into the local paper of course, but the Canadian Press never took it up, there being a couple of dreadful air crashes, an African revolution and a volcanic eruption to distract them at the time. It was, however, for us, a matter of some seriousness. The very day after the meeting half a dozen women, some with small children in attendance, picketted Doherty's Store bearing placards, which read variously "Ban Jelly Babies," "Protect the newborn" and, rather obscurely, "Ritual Murder." Mr. Doherty himself came to the door and asked what it was all about. He was told that jelly babies were obscene travesties of ordinary babies, that they were an incitement to infanticide, that they were degrading to women (and presumably to babies) and that they could not be tolerated in the community. Lucia Griddle, who works in the library, referred to witches sticking pins in dolls and to pagan customs, at which one of her colleagues looked a little blank.

"But," said Mr. Doherty, in tones as reasonable as he could muster, "they're sold all over town. They're very popular. Especially the black ones." It was difficult to say which of the three statements agitated the group more. They went into a sort of huddle, and decided to have another meeting straightaway. They downed their placards and went off to Lavinia Blades' house, which was nearest, and there they prepared a plan of action. There were several schools of thought, or, rather, schools of emphasis. One considered that the first thing to do was discover where jelly babies came from and picket the factory, but it was suspected that the factory was far away in Ontario, and perhaps even in the States—or England someone said, trying to give the thing an international flavour.

"I remember," she said, "eating them in England when I was a girl." Then she blushed.

"At least," said another, "we must get something in the paper, and we must picket every store that sells them.

"But how to get into the paper?" enquired Lavinia.

"A public meeting," cried Maud (she was a great one for public meetings). "They'll have to report that."

Few public meetings in Centreville are well attended, but this one was an exception to the rule. There were easily fifty people there, including baffled husbands, and a number of storekeepers who wanted to know what the fuss was about. There were also a contingent from the Pro-Choice group who saw the whole thing as an anti-abortion issue, two born-again Christians, whose attitudes suggested that the rebirth had been only partly successful, and a large young woman who sported a button reading "Black is Beautiful," which, in the context of the situation, seemed a little ambiguous. I sat at the back beside the local reporter, who had a notepad, and was obliged to put out his cigarette when Maud, who was naturally chairman, or should I say chairperson, opened the proceedings by announcing, "There will be no smoking at this meeting."

The first speaker was Lucia Griddle, who told us that jelly babies were relics of pagan times, referred abstrusely to human sacrifices in Peru, to bones of children being found under the foundation stones of ancient buildings, and to cannibalism. She said, "Thou shall not kill" several times with a slight squeak in her voice. She was followed by Marcia DeLisle who spoke of the Importance of Home Environment, the need to perceive Babies as Tender and Loving (she was childless), and then continued to talk of the Wickedness of Selling War Toys to impressionable children. "Guns, Tanks, Rayguns, Soldiers, Rumballs" she said, (but I think she meant Rambos) "are everywhere. Our children are taught that killing is good. Our boys are persuaded to be killers. This," she said, "is a country of Peace. Canada has always been a country of Peace. In Canada," she said, in a final peroration, "we do not Eat Babies."

There was a scattering of applause at this last statement, some of it, I fear, sardonic.

The third speaker had to overcome some muttered conversation among the audience. She spoke of Unhealthy Appetites. She said that candies rotted children's teeth and that powdered sugar caused cancer, and gelatine clogged the bowels. She seemed, indeed, to have rather lost the point, and was brought to a full stop by the large girl with the button who cried out in stentorian tones, "What about the blacks?" The speaker took one slightly frenzied glance around the room, mumbled something, and sat down with a gesture at Maud, who, after all, was conducting the meeting.

"Make your point," said Maud. The girl made her point. She said it was a matter of racism. It was well known that the black babies had their heads bitten off first. The other colours were simply a front intended to conceal the racist intention of the symbolism. "This is a racist country," she informed us. "How many blacks are there in Parliament? How many are there on the Supreme Court? How many are there on the City Council of Centreville?" Nobody had the answers to the first two questions. She answered the third one herself. "None!" she declaimed and sat down. So far as I knew there were no blacks in Centreville whatsoever.

Maud, sidetracked, attempted to make the point. "There are no or few black residents in Centreville to stand for election."

"Precisely," said the girl, "Centreville bans blacks."

I could hear the placard in her voice. The Mayor, who had been hiding somewhere across to the left, stood up. "Centreville is an interracial city," he stated, "all . . . er . . . colours and creeds are welcome here."

Maud slammed the table with her hand. She had forgotten to bring a gavel. "Next point," she said.

The elder of the two pro-choicers stood up. "Women must have the freedom to choose whether or not to give birth," she said. "They are the only ones who can choose. It is their responsibility, and a part of their function and inheritance as women."

"They could use contraceptives," said someone nastily from the centre of the hall, and one of the born-againers cried out with passion, "Sex is Sin!" The meeting was clearly getting out of hand.

Maud, with a grand gesture, said, "We all seem agreed that the sale of jelly babies should be prohibited. Can I have a show of hands?" A few hands rose, but the manager of Shoppe-Qik rose more quickly.

"That would be a restriction of trade," he said. "It would be an attack on the rights of the business community which serves you all, and whose taxes pay for the upkeep of this splendid city and ensure its prosperity."

"By selling war toys?" asked someone, and "By killing babies?" enquired a harsher voice.

The Manager took a deep breath. "If my business is in any way affected," he stated, "I will have the members of picket lines arrested by the police for causing a public nuisance."

"You always call in the police," cried the girl with the button. "The police are the hired hands of racialism. Think of Alabama in the Sixties. Think of South Africa today. Picket! Boycott!! Protest! Stand up for the Rights of Minorities, for the Rights of Women."

Maud slammed the table once again. "Order," she called. "All viewpoints have now been heard. I want a show of hands." She did not say for what, but some hands rose and the meeting broke up.

The paper did not come out for two days and during that period the population held its breath, except for those people who were making placards. When the paper did come out, it not only provided a long report of the meeting, replete with misquotations and typographical errors, but also a large announcement, stating "A Protest March Will Take Place" on the following day. The March was to begin at Doherty's corner store, proceed past the Shoppe-Qik, The Kozy Kandy Store, and Lee's corner Grocery to the Town Hall steps, where the throng would be addressed by Maud, as the newly elected president of "The Women's Infant Protection Society" (WIPS).

There was, however, a second notice from a group calling itself "Women's Choice" (WC) which announced that it would present a petition to the Mayor in support of Freedom of Choice and then march through the town along a different route, which only crossed the path of the other group outside the Shoppe-Qik. I bumped into the Police Sergeant just after I had read these two notices, and waved the paper at him. "Yes," he said, "we gave them permits. We had to. The Mayor's wife is a pro-choicer and his sister-in-law is one of the others. He's drafted a couple of specials to help us out, just in case, but after all, they shouldn't meet. One lot's due at the Shoppe-Qik at two thirty and the other at three. That gives them plenty of time." I did not like to disquiet him; I decided I might do a little shopping at the Shoppe-Qik myself that afternoon.

It all began, I was told, quite decorously. The WIPS group marched solemnly in front of the stores, and handed out badly inked pamphlets. The WCs delivered a petition bearing twenty names to the Mayor and set off with placards announcing "Free Women to Choose"; "Birthright is a Freedom not a Condemnation"; "A Woman's Child is a Woman's Choice"; and a smaller notice carried by an aggressive looking young woman with red hair whom nobody dared tackle and everybody avoided looking at, saying simply, "Down With Motherhood." She, I assumed, was not childless.

On the corner of Burke Street and First Avenue, at around two thirty, I waited with some interest. The WIPS were behind time, as I was sure they would be, for they intended to stop to wave placards and hand out leaflets at various points along their route. The WCs were, however, a little ahead of time as I had thought they might be, for they had no pamphlets to hand out, and did not pause on their march. It was around ten to three when the WIPS arrived at Shoppe-Qik and they paraded up and down in front of the First Avenue entrance chanting "Jelly Babies Must Go" over and over again. It was somewhat repetitious. Indeed, one character in the small crowd that had gathered on the other side of the street struck up "Lloyd George Knows My Father," presumably in order to enliven the proceedings.

The WCs were by now almost at the intersection. I was interested to observe that the girl with the button had allied herself with this cause rather than the other one. Her placard read "Down With The Establishment." The two policemen in the middle of the intersection looked nervous, and one of them began making traffic direction signals to stop the WIPS proceeding and urge the WCs across in safety. Nobody paid any attention. The groups stood facing one another; Maud at the head of one, and the girl with the button at the head of the other. She clearly saw herself as a born leader. Maud gestured for her followers to recommence their chant, and then, to everyone's surprise, she ran quickly into the Shoppe-Qik. The button girl looked after her, and seemed to guess something I could not guess. With equal swiftness she placed her placard in the hands of a follower and entered the store by the side entrance, emerging only a second or two after Maud. Both had big old fashioned jars of jelly babies in their hands.

Maud silenced her group with a wave, and shouting "These are the symbols of degradation" dipped her hand into the jar, threw a handful of babies onto the street, and ground them with her heel. The button girl took a deep breath, dipped into her own jar, took out a handful of infants and hurled them at Maud. I do not know whether the Manager of Shoppe-Qik had contrived to lay in extra stock on a premonition, but in moments members of both groups were in the shop, then out again, with jars and bags of jelly babies in their hands, and they were hurling them with ferocity. The policemen ran forward. One of them got one in the eye, I do not know from whom, and it slowed him down a good bit. His partner skidded on the babies Maud had trampled and landed on his back.

The button girl, having run out of babies, advanced, wielding her placard with intent to damage. Marcia De Lisle, with exemplary dexterity, forgot all about Loving Tenderness, and tripped her up, and then the fight was on.

The Great Jelly Baby Riot of Centreville did not make the national press. It did not, as a matter of fact, even make the local press, for the mayor spoke to the editor and the editor spoke to the reporter, and they reprinted an article on Our Local Wildlife instead.

The following weeks were rather dull. Maud's WIPS seemed to fade away, and her Women's Group lost one or two of its weaker members. The WCs were also unobservable. It was indeed several weeks before Joyce Tregeseal, at a Women's Group Meeting, pointed out that more than eighty percent of the books in the local library were written by men, and that the only woman writers at all well represented were writers of books for children. "Are Canadian women to be deprived of their Right To Speak?" she enquired. "Are we to be Muzzled?" But that, as they say, is another story.

The Good Row

IT WOULD HAVE BEEN FUNNY, REALLY, if it wasn't so hurtful, though I've mostly got over the hurt by now. I do get a bit lonely though. It isn't so much living alone—or almost alone—it's the way some of them still avoid me when I leave the house to go shopping or anything at all, come to that. Of course, it's a small place and everyone knows everybody, and knows everybody's business too, so it's not very surprising. But what maddens me—or used to madden me—is that there was no evidence whatsoever. How could there be? I didn't do it. Moreover, I was miles away at the time, and I'm dead certain it was an accident in any case. Still, people around here are suspicious. "No smoke without fire"—that sort of thing—and I admit we had a hell of a row the night before, but there wasn't much new about that. We actually enjoyed having rows. There, I've admitted it, as I never admitted it to him or him to me. Not in those days, at any rate. You can't really have a good stand-up knock-down cursing scrap if you let on you're enjoying it all the time. You're liable to laugh, and that would spoil it. You can laugh the next morning, of course. That's all in the game. But you mustn't laugh at the time.

Well, I do admit it was one of our noisier rows. It was his bright idea of drowning me out by beating the old tin bath from the shed with a ladle that made it the noisiest. I had to admire him for that. I was in full voice, and I've got a big voice, and I could usually drown him out eventually, though he had a few tricks too, like sitting down right in the middle of the argument and whispering his insults so that I had to stop shouting to appreciate them properly. That was sneaky. Oh, but he was always the sneaky one. Still is, in a manner of speaking.

I can't remember what the row was about. It doesn't really matter much. They all say it was about money. Perhaps it was, I can't remember. It wasn't about a woman anyway. Not even they could believe that. It may have started with just simple irritation. He had a way of scraping his plate after dinner that really irritated me—he made the plate squeak somehow—I don't know how he did it. Or maybe it was because I'd thrown the *Macleans* away before he'd read Fotheringham; he could get in a fury about that any time.

I'm making it sound as if we were always quarrelling. Well, we weren't, whatever people say. It was only once or twice a month that we had a bust-up. Letting off steam really. And who wouldn't want to let off steam sometimes after a couple of weeks in that damn factory. Mindless that work is, mindless. We used to read a lot, of course. Nobody believes me about that, but we did. And we watched TV. Maybe it was the TV we fought about. We could do that easily enough. But once every now and then with nothing on the box and the books beginning to pall, one of us—maybe both— would get an itch for a fight. It was a relief I can tell you, a real relief. And, as I say, we enjoyed it.

That particular night, the night he got the tin bath out of the shed, we were in rattling good form. I was staggered by that tin bath, I can tell you. But you can't keep a good man down and I remembered the old motor horn I'd found years back and put in a drawer. An honest to god Klaxon it was, and so I answered him with that. It surprised him, even awed him, I think, but he didn't show it. How could he? It roused him though, I can tell you that. So there we were banging and hooting and shouting, and really living it up, and when the moment came to stop we did it in the usual fashion. We tended to take it in turns. It wasn't planned. It was like a game, you know. One of us would make one last enormous roar, and slam away to bed with the last great insult. It was his turn that night. He deserved it. I wish I'd thought of that tin bath. He hurled it down on the floor with one hell of a crash and shouted out "I swear, I'll kill you, I'll kill you!" at the top of his voice, and exited, slamming the door of his room.

I sat down, hot and exhausted, and shaking a bit. These things always take it out of you. Then I got a glass and some ice and gave myself a double and went off to bed. I knew that once I was well away he'd come in and do the same thing. It was a routine you see, a routine. And at breakfast we'd be laughing. We'd done it all so many times, and it just made our friendship stronger. You have to believe that. They didn't, but you must. They thought that "I'll kill you" stuff was for real. What's worse, they think I yelled it, not him. They can't even tell our voices apart, or whoever was passing at that time— around midnight it was—couldn't tell them apart.

Now maybe you can understand why there was such a fuss when he was killed. It was two days later. I didn't kill him, though. I have to make you understand that. He did it to himself. It was on a Sunday morning they found him. We had a big stone jar on a ledge up over the kitchen door. Full of salt it was; he was going to salt some runner beans—you know how you do it—a layer of salt, a layer of beans—it's easy enough, and he likes that sort of thing. He used to hang hams as well. That was one of his pleasures. Well, someone saw the kitchen door standing open and his hand sticking out onto the step, and they went over and there he was with his skull stoved in. The jar had fallen on him and sent him against the door and knocked it open. There was blood everywhere, they said at the inquest, and the idiot who found the body said he thought immediately that it was murder. He enjoyed saying that. The coroner and the police sergeant tried to shut him up, but it was too late, and then people got up and said we were always quarrelling, and I'd been heard threatening to kill him only two days earlier.

Well, that did it. It was no use their being told that I spent that Saturday night at my cousin's place, and had stayed over, and that I was fifty miles away. "There are such things as cars," they said, "aren't there? And he could have got out the window, driven over and done it easy. He fixed himself an alibi," they said. Well, they made such a nuisance of themselves the police went and talked to my cousin, and he said not only was I there all night but they were sure I was because the baby had had a bad night and they had to keep getting up to see to it and every time they did that they saw me on the living room couch. "And he was snoring," said my cousin's wife, and with some bitterness, or so the sergeant told me. She thought it was my snoring that bothered the baby.

You can't talk sense to some folk, though, and I got pretty fed up with the situation. Everyone, as I say, avoided me. Even at work. And they kept it up too. I'd have left town but jobs are hard to come by, and anyway I don't mind so much now. Now that he's back. We never did have too much use for other folk anyway.

I didn't realize. I'm sorry. I should have told you that first of all. Yes, he came back. It was about a month later, and I was watching the TV when the channel suddenly changed. I couldn't understand it. It just switched over. I put it back of course. Then it switched over again, and this time I heard a chuckle. I looked round, wondering what the hell was going on, and there he was sitting in his old chair, and grinning at me. Well, I was scared to begin with. I said, "I didn't do it. You know I didn't do it."

"Of course you didn't, you great thick," he said. "Don't I know that? Though you could have rigged that jar, you know, come to think of it," and he scratched his head thoughtfully. He spoke as clearly as you or me, and he looked as solid as you do, and it was so natural I started to get mad straightaway.

"You lying layabout," I said. "You're just trying to pick a fight. And keep your hands off the TV too, you great stupid bugger." I'd no sooner said it than I realized that I was exactly right. He *was* picking a fight. He wanted a row. Well, I didn't quite know how to handle it. I mean, having a row with your mate is one thing, but having a row with a ghost is quite another. I'd never heard of it. Most of the ghosts I'd heard of came in with moans and rattles and accused you of some crimes or other, and you were supposed to cower away from them in mortal terror, and the next day your hair turned white and you went to the funny farm or cut your throat or something. At least that's how I heard it.

"Thick, that's what you are," he said. "Letting all those people out there get away with thinking you killed me. As if you could. You haven't the guts to kill a kitten."

Well, that struck a sore spot. He once asked me to drown some kittens that had come to our tabby, and I hadn't had the stomach for it. Nor had he, come to that, so we gave them all away—with a bit of bribery in some cases. But he'd made the point first and you can't get up a good fight with an "It wasn't me, it was you" sort of argument, so I went on to something else.

"You weren't so tough when you passed out at the blood clinic," I said, and I'd got him there. I didn't think a ghost could turn red; I thought they were stuck with being pallid and grey, but he turned red all right, and the row was on.

It was a lovely row. He didn't get the tin bath this time. I'm not sure he could handle it. In fact, he tried to pick up a bottle to hammer on the table and his hand went through it, which gave me a point or two. "You're nothing but a fucking ghost," I shouted, "can't even pick up a bottle."

He took a deep breath and shouted back, "At least I'm not going to die of snivelling old age with my nose in a whisky bottle and my pension up my arse!"

I wasn't sure what he meant about the pension, but it sounded good and that's all that mattered. Anyway, I had the advantage, and I remembered the Klaxon and started in with that. What could he do? Well, the old bugger turned the TV on full blast to drown me out—just gave it a look and it went on. So there I was on the horn, him on the TV, and as it was my turn there came a point when I threw the Klaxon to the floor and shouted, "I'll . . . I'll . . . " and I was stymied and he was beginning to laugh at me which wasn't right at all. Then I got it. "I'll exorcise you!" I shrieked, and slammed off to bed.

I gave him time to go back to wherever he had to go before I stole out for my drink of scotch. I wondered about breakfast. I hoped he'd be there. He wasn't though. I suppose breakfasts aren't in a ghost's line—fading at cock-crow and all that stuff. Still, I pretended he was there, and that was almost as good. Come dusk that night, he turned

up again. We didn't row, of course. I let him have the TV pro-
gramme he wanted and we watched it together. It was just like old
times. Then just before I turned in, he said "I can't keep it up you
know."

"Keep what up?"

"Well, visiting. There's a limit. After I've been dead a month or
so I have to make it permanent."

That saddened me. It really did. "But there's time for at least
one good row before you go," I said.

"Sure," he said. "When it's right. When it's the time."

Well, it was a couple of weeks later that the time came, and we
had the best row yet. He'd thought up a few tricks to irritate me.
For one thing he'd dodge—sort of fade away in one place and
come up behind me and whisper in my ear. I'd thought of one or
two as well. I knew I couldn't hurt him, because he wasn't really
solid, so I threw things. We'd thrown stuff before. Who needs to
break up their own crockery? But this was a special occasion, so I
threw everything. Oh, it was a great night, and when it was time,
and his turn to go, he yelled out, as his parting shot, "I'll Haunt
you!" and I broke all the rules and burst out laughing, and so did
he, and he didn't slam out. I don't think he could in any case. He
wasn't solid enough for a good slam. He sat down at a table, and I
got the whisky and I drank for both of us.

Well, that was the last time, or almost the last, but you know I'm
not as lonely as I was. They still avoid me in the street, but word
got around that I've gone a bit crazy, smashed up my kitchen and
so forth, and they say it's because of the way they've treated me. So,
it's still a bit hurtful, but not half as bad as it was. And every now
and then, about once a month or so, he doesn't exactly come back
for a full dress row, but the TV changes channels all by itself, and I

hear a chuckle, and a whisper, "You stupid old bugger," and, you know, I shout out, "I'll exorcise you." It's our joke. And it's as good a way as any of passing the time 'til we can have another good row somewhere else.

In Camera

I'M A PHOTOGRAPHER.
That's one reason I like your cottage. That back room is just ideal for a dark room—it's got the sink and everything.

I have a little studio downtown, and I do portraits and fashion stuff and things for magazines. Not Playboy stuff, you understand, at least not usually. Some bathing suits, of course. I'm pretty good, though I say so myself. And I make a decent living—or I wouldn't be able to afford that cottage.

Yes, I know, it's the going rate, and I'm not objecting. And I'm glad your uncle was a photographer. It makes it feel more comfortable in a way. And it's quiet. But there's just one thing. Would you mind terribly if I take a photograph of it before I decide? I could print it up tonight and let you know tomorrow. I know that isn't a normal request—but in some respects I'm not, well, normal. Not anything really awful, you understand. But, I suppose you could say eccentric. I just have to do that.

I have to photograph it from all angles. The inside as well.

Photographs sometimes show things that the eye can't see—at least that most eyes can't see. It won't take me long.

All right. I can understand you wondering a bit. I'll tell you about it if you like. Only in confidence, please.

It began about six months ago. I'd taken a family group in the studio—mother, father, two kids—nothing special about it. And that night when I developed the film I found a little white spot on the negs. On all of them. And all in the same place. Now that was funny. A little spot on one could be just a flaw in the film or something, but on all of them didn't make sense. And the spot wasn't on any other neg in the roll. Well, I printed the things, and I got rid of the spot on the prints themselves. It was no problem. But it puzzled me. I couldn't understand it at all. I make my customers pick up the prints personally from the studio. I have a secretary-receptionist to handle all that kind of thing, books and accounts and bills and so forth. It's really quite a decent business. I happened to be out front, though, when the father of the family came in and so I asked after the family.

"Had a spot of bother," he said. "Charlie"—that was the son—"was out skateboarding and he broke his leg." Quite suddenly the negs flashed into my mind.

"Which leg?" I asked.

"The right one," he said, and then, "Are you feeling all right?" I must have turned pale. I said something about always getting upset when children were hurt, which I am actually, but it wasn't that at all. You see, the little white dot had been on Charlie's right leg.

Now, things like this do happen, and I know there are stories about cameras photographing things that aren't really there—ghosts and stuff—but I'd never expected it to happen to me. Anyway, I got over it fairly quickly, and I didn't tell anyone, and it wasn't for another little while that it happened again. This time it was a very pretty girl, in a bathing costume. I think she was going in for a beauty competition or something, and it was her right arm. She collected the print with her arm in a sling. I didn't see her myself, but Penny—that's my receptionist—told me and said it was a shame wasn't it and she was such a pretty girl, and I said yes it was a shame, and I really felt bad about it, but what could I say, I couldn't tell her. What was there to tell? I changed cameras just in case.

In fact I locked that camera away, and used another one that day for a chap who wanted some publicity photos. You know the kind. Very solemn and stern and authoritative, and from the waist up so you couldn't tell how short he was. After the session he left me a medium size poster showing another photograph of him and said he'd like the print exactly that size. It made it easier to reproduce, and cheaper, if it didn't have to be enlarged or reduced. The poster told me he was an alderman. There was a local election coming up. He picked up the print the next day, and there was a muffler round his neck. It wasn't a cold day either, though it was still early Spring. He had laryngitis, he whispered. The white dot had been on his throat.

I guess I was in a bit of a state by then.

It wasn't the camera at all. It couldn't be. I thought it might be the studio itself, but I'd had no trouble before this and so it didn't seem likely. I told myself I was overtired and that might have something to do with it, but I'd got too many bookings to even think about taking time off that week, so I had to go on. And that night the negs showed nothing. The next night, though, I got another spot. It was on a man's body. Just over the heart. He didn't collect the print; his wife did, a week or so later. She told my receptionist he was recovering quite well. It had only been a minor heart attack.

I did close the studio for a week after that. I was living in an apartment then, in a big house, and the walls were paper thin, but my neighbours were quiet enough and I didn't play loud music myself so it was all very comfortable. Anyway I couldn't stop work entirely, so I decided that for a while I wouldn't take any photographs, I'd just print up some old negs, and make exhibition prints. I had quite a lot I hadn't had time to deal with as well as I'd have liked, and there was a photography show coming up in July and I thought I'd like to be represented. As I told you, I usually just do studio stuff—portraits and so forth—but I enjoy landscape work, too, and taking old buildings, and things like that. Well, I'd got a really marvellous shot of the old Bilborough Place, an old house, built around 1890 I'd say, and I thought this would do just fine for the show. The heritage boys would love it. So I got out the neg and made the prints and put them in the sink to develop, and felt relieved. I turned them over in the sink a couple of times to be sure that everything was going well. It's surprising how nervous I was getting.

Perhaps you're right. It isn't really surprising at all. But I was certainly jittery. With reason as it happened. I had just turned my back for a second when there was a sort of flash of light from the sink and I turned around and the prints—there were three of them—were floating on the surface and burning up. I screamed. I couldn't help it. I screamed. And I ran out of the apartment yelling "fire," stupidly really—I mean the only thing on fire was in the sink—it was about as dangerous as a candle flame. It brought the neighbours running and they dashed into the apartment with me and one had picked up the fire extinguisher, but by that time the fire was out. It wasn't only that, though. There was no sign of it at all. And there were three prints sitting there in the sink quite harmlessly. I apologized. I said I'd had a nightmare. They looked at me a bit oddly. I mean, I was fully dressed and had clearly been in the darkroom so how could I possibly have had a nightmare? They went away grumbling, and I did no more work that night and I fished the prints out of the sink, and they were all black, every one of them. There was nothing to be seen at all. The next morning in the newspaper—perhaps you remember—it was the old Bilborough place—it had burned down.

Yes. You're right. It burned right down to the foundations. Thank God nobody was hurt. It was a terrible loss, really, though. And I was completely shattered. Still, I managed to pull myself together after a while and tried to reason the thing out. The fire in the sink had given me the clue. There hadn't been a spot on the neg at all, you see. And so whatever happened had happened in the printing process, not in the camera itself. And so maybe all those white spots had arrived during developing. It was all in the processing. I took my courage in both hands and decided to experiment. The next week, back at work, I did not develop or print myself, I sent the stuff out to a friend. I told him my darkroom was being reorganized. It cost a bit extra of course, which was a nuisance, and he wasn't, to be truthful, as good at producing prints as me, but there were no white spots on any of the prints or the negs, so I was relieved.

I went on like that for a while, but business began to fall off. The prints just lacked the extra touch, you know. They were good, but they weren't first class. I had to risk it again. So one Friday I decided I'd process just one roll myself. I wanted to, anyway. It was a bit of an experiment. My daughter's request. She wanted me to give her a portrait of myself. Well, she lives at the other end of things, in Halifax to be exact, and I'd asked her what she wanted for her birthday and she said this was it. Very flattering. I wasn't too nervous about doing it, really, though I admit to a qualm or two as I fixed up the camera and the remote control thing. Still, I'd heard somewhere or other that one of the things a clairvoyant cannot do is see his—or her—own future, however good they are at other people's. So, as I say, I set everything up, and I really went to town.

There were some tricks I'd always meant to try out and hadn't the nerve to do for anyone else, and I suppose I was too cheap to hire a model. Not big tricks, you understand—just lighting effects—like some of the ones you get in old movies—expressionist stuff, and that sort of thing. Shadows in odd places. Spotlights on the mouth or the eyes. That sort of thing. They were full-face, though. I had this idea of keeping the one pose, and only altering it with the light. Besides it made it easier. I did it in a chair and I fixed a couple of nails in the chair back so I could feel them touching the same place on my neck each time.

It was difficult doing it all by myself as you can imagine, and I really worked hard. I took a whole Sunday to do it. Thirty-six exposures. It was quite an effort. When I started processing I admit I offered up a little prayer to whatever god of photography there might be up there or out there somewhere, and when I got the negs out of the tank I think my hand shook a little. Still, there was nothing for it. I had to look.

I started to look at them from the top of the roll, in the order in which they'd been shot. Of course the negs were small and I couldn't see anything much, so I stuck them in the enlarger.

In case you don't know about an enlarger, it's a sort of projector. It projects the neg onto sensitized paper to the size you want, and that's how you get prints. As big as you like, according to the adjustment you make, and the size of the enlarger itself.

Well, I blew the first one up quite a bit and could still see very little, but there was just a pin prick of a spot on my forehead, very faint. I told myself it meant nothing and moved on to the next one. This time there was another really small spot, but it wasn't quite in the same place. It seemed almost as if it had moved. I began to feel scared. I remembered the broken leg and the heart attack and the laryngitis, not to forget the burned down old house, and said "brain tumour" to myself, and then, ridiculously, "Not a bit of it. Just a headache." Well, that bit was right anyway. I *was* getting a headache. Still, I moved on, and so did the spot. Not very far, just a little way. It was on the forehead still.

After I'd gone through half a dozen I realized that the spots were not shifting about randomly. They were more like those dots you get in the funnies from time to time. You know, "Draw lines between these dots and discover what Timmy Topknot sees," or something like that. I couldn't work out how to link them at first. Then I got the idea. I put a sheet of fresh paper on the enlarger platform, and then I projected number one. And I got a pin and made a hole in the paper through the spot. Then I did it with the second one. See how it works? Well, after I'd done the whole film I switched on the light and linked up the dots as a kid would. They didn't make sense. They seemed to be random. After all, the kids' dots in the funnies had numbers on them, and these didn't. I tried all sorts of different arrangements. After a bit I decided that maybe the order I'd shot them in mattered, so I did it all over again and I linked them up with a pencil as I pricked them out, but all I got was a jumble. I really had got a headache then, so I gave up and just printed the things as usual and decided I'd take the dots out the next day when the prints were dry. I kept the paper with the dots on though, and went on trying to make sense of them.

It took a week or two, as I remember, before I got a sort of picture, but I'm not at all sure it made sense. It depends on how you look at things. I reasoned it out, actually. It came to me one day standing in the street outside the optician's. There was a big picture of an eye, and I thought immediately that that must be the answer, and it was. I linked up the dots again and, sure enough, that's what it was. An eye. And, of course, on the prints it would be right in the middle of my forehead. The third eye! The pineal gland! Well, I felt better after that. At least I wasn't going to have a brain tumour or something. I'd been a bit concerned, as you might have guessed.

That's all there is to it really. Or almost all. Now, when I develop film or make prints I wear a black toque that comes right down over my forehead and I have no trouble at all. Still, it's been useful from time to time, I must admit. It does give me hints about things. That's why I want to photograph your cottage. There might be something about it that I should know; it seems to work on things as well as people. After all, it worked on the old building, didn't it! So it should work on your cottage.

You're right, of course. I have experimented, naturally. How could I help it? But it doesn't turn out always the way I expect. It doesn't interpret after all, it just sort of indicates. It saw a spot on my car the other week, on the hood, so I drove it to the garage and had it overhauled. There was nothing wrong at all. I was surprised. The next day when I went out to drive it to work there was a big bird dropping on the exact place it had shown me.

And another time I decided really to test the thing out and I photographed two bowling teams. They were due to face each other in a championship. Well, the first team had so spots at all, but the second team had several. One woman had one on her foot, and one on her head as well, and a second had one right on her eye, and a third had quite a big spot on her leg. It looked to me like they would hardly be in a fit state to play at all, much less win. Well, I have to admit that I laid a bet or two and sat watching, feeling full of confidence, and even a bit smug, especially as the team I'd bet against kept doing so well. "Wait for it," I told myself. "Something's going to happen." Something did happen. They won. I could hardly believe it. And I was still in a daze when the cup was presented—it was a big silver gilt thing—heavy—probably electroplated lead. Well, the team leader took the cup with a bright smile, lost her grip and dropped it on her foot. She gave a yowl of pain and hopped a bit but bent down to pick it up at the exact moment one of her team, another woman, bent down to do the same thing; their heads connected with an almighty crack and the second woman reeled backwards and cannoned into a third woman who fell over a chair and when it was all sorted out the three of them were in a fine state of confusion. One was rubbing her head and limping, the other had a hand clasped over her eye, and the third was massaging her leg.

I gave up after that, until one day I was printing a series of shots I'd taken of the preparations for a country fair. I do these outdoorsy things from time to time. It's a change, and, anyway, these were commissioned. Well there was a sawing competition and I took some shots of people practising and one of the men, a big burly chap, came out with spots on every finger of his right hand. I was scared. It could only mean one thing. He was going to lose his fingers. I touched up the print and gave it to the people who'd commissioned it, and I positively raced around to see this chap. I felt I had to warn him. I told him he would lose his fingers. Heaven help me, I told him I was psychic. He was in his backyard at the time, oiling his saw, and he got crosser and crosser. I don't know what set him off. It may have been the word psychic. He wasn't keen on things like that, I'd say. Anyway, he got really mad, and I made the mistake of laying my hand on his saw to emphasize how sharp the teeth were, and he took a swing at me, and got me right on the jaw, and I went down and out like a light. When I woke up he was sitting on the back steps cursing. He had broken his fingers.

So you see I won't do it any longer. I wear the toque all the time. And please don't ask me to forecast horse races or anything. Just let me take a few shots of the cottage before I decide, as a sort of precaution. And don't tell anyone about all this, will you? I mean this conversation, all of it, has to be in camera.

The Colloquium

IT'S IGNORANCE THAT'S BEHIND IT ALL. Ignorance is the creature. Do you know what I'm telling you? There's devil a bit of decent education about these days. You don't get the Prime Minister standing up and spouting Latin as they used. Pro Bono Publico, all that kind of stuff. And if you so much as drop a word about Diodorus Sicylus in a pub you're likely to be asked if it grows in sandy soil, and is it perennial. It's disheartening to a man like me, I can tell you. Not that I'm College educated, mind you. I wouldn't set foot in one of them places. They don't educate any longer. It's all computering these days, and was it Leonardo Bellini or Samuel Botticelli did this picture, put a cross in the right box. No, I'm a Carnegie man. I mean the public library. Wet or shine, day on day, you'll find me there, studying. That's another thing. Specialization. I don't believe in it. William Burton didn't specialize when he put together the Analogy of Melancholy; he got everything in, English, Latin, the lot. No, the thing to do is broaden your horizons, extend yourself. Myself, I spend a powerful

lot of time with the Encyclopaedia. This last week I did Anthropol-
ogy, Lever Strauss, Ronald Fraser, Ruth Benedictine, that gang.
Next week it'll be Philosophy again, Neetche, Shopehower, Aris-
totle, all them. This week it's Ettimology, with the old Oxford
Dictionary, the big job with the little print. Hard on the eyes that
one, and you need a bit of muscle to heave it about.

I was telling all this to a young woman in the coffee shop the
other morning. I take a coffee break now and then to let things
settle down in my head. She says I'm an Ortodiedack. And a Polly
something or other. She talked a bit quick and I couldn't catch it
all. She said were my friends as keen on studying as me. I had to tell
her I didn't have too many friends, had no time for them with all
the studying. It's in the Carnegie at opening time, coffee break, a
bit of lunch at the pub, back again, tea-break, back again, a bite of
supper, and on 'til closing time and off to the digs. When the
Carnegie's shut on holidays I do a bit of light stuff at home.
Penguin books, that sort of thing. Non-fiction, though. I don't go
for fiction. That's not educating, really. It's all made-up stuff. You
can't rely on it. My Dad wouldn't let fiction in the house. Work of
the Devil he called it. Well, I can't say I agree with that. I'm a bit
sceptical about that lad, horns and hoofs and that stuff. It's out-
murdered. I dipped into poetry a bit a few years ago, put my toe in
the water you might say, but it wasn't the thing. No, it's Ettymo-
logy, Philosophy, History, Geography, Geology, Paleontology,
that class of thing for me. That's really education. You get to know
a lot that road.

Well, this young woman said I did wrong keeping it all to myself.
She said I shouldn't hide my light under a bushel, that I should have
a few chaps round of an evening and form a study group. A sort of
club, she said, like they used to have in the old days, and I should give

a talk about what I'd studied and all that. Soon as she said it I felt bursting with stuff to talk about. There was so much, I didn't know where to begin, so I asked her. We kicked it about a bit and settled on Plato. There's a lot to talk about in that lad.

The next job was to get a study group put together. I don't drink much myself, just a jar at lunch and one or two of an evening, but I got a few in. I wouldn't get the group at all without that. First of all I asked Charlie, the doorman at the Carnegie. I see him more often than most. But he wasn't for it at all. Then I tried Mike at the Sally Ann where I get my Penguins. He said No, but why not try Ted over at the paperbacks. He was a great reader and would do anything for a free beer. Ted was willing, and he said he'd bring his mate, Ron. I only got one other. That was Paddy from the room down the hall. I thought about the landlady, but I couldn't afford gin and, anyway, I doubt she'd ever shoved her nose in a real book. Romance was more her line and things about nurses. I'd seen them lying by the bottle when I took the rent. It was a small enough lot for a study group, but big trees from little acorns grow as my Dad used to say when he put my Saturday sixpence in the money-box.

Well, we got settled down to it that Thursday, Ted and Ron on the bed together because they were mates, and Paddy on one chair and me on the other, and I'd borrowed a couple of extra glasses from the landlady so we were all set. "This evening," I said, "I'm going to start off with a bit about Plato."

"You mean that dog?" said Ron, a bit puzzled.

"No," I said, "that's Pluto. He was called after the kings of the underworld. They called it Hades, the ancient Greeks did. We call it Hell."

"It's a Hell of a name for a King," said Ted. "Was he a dog then?"

"Of course not," I told him. "The dog in that shop was Cerberellum. He had three heads, and sat on the other side of the river from where you'd be standing to get across." I could see that there'd be other questions, so I put on a bit of speed. "Plato was an ancient Greek philosopher, and he had a great thing about the Republic."

"I was in the War," said Paddy. "King and Country and to hell with the Republic. Ulster will fight and Ulster will be right." I think he'd had a jar or two before he got to the group.

"This wasn't a real Republic," I said. "He made it up. There were three sorts of people. First off there was the Philosophers and they were the kings."

"You can't have kings in a republic," said Ted. "That's what republic means: no kings."

"Well, they were statesmen, sort of members of the cabinet, not real kings," I said. "And then there were the Police and the Army, and then there were all the rest that did the work and got the food and stuff for the higher ups."

"He didn't make that bit up," said Ted. "He got that right."

"And you got to be on the top by being full up with virtue and education," I said.

"You're codding us," said Ted. "Virtue and education. Them fellers? Would you look at them! It might be all right for Greeks, but it's not like that here."

"There's nothing wrong with Greeks," said Ron. "I had a Greek brother-in-law once. Fantastic cook he was. On the old P&O line."

"I was on them for a bit," Paddy said, brightening up and helping himself to another bottle. "A steward. The chief was a scouse. Little feller with black hair. Used to whistle through his teeth."

"My brother-in-law came from Athens."

"Like Plato." I put in. "Plato came from Athens."

"Could he cook?" Ron asked. "Those Greeks are great cooks. My brother-in-law did something called Musica that would really put a lining on your stomach."

"Music," said Paddy, "that's the lad! Would you ever know the Orange Flute?"

"Mozart?" I said.

"No," he said. "I had it off my Dad in Derry. You'll get it after a bit," and off he started.

Ted got the tune right away, and Ron was only a bit behind, then the landlady came up, and I told her we'd been talking about Plato. She said, "That's not talk, that's singing and there's rules in this house." Ted swallowed the last drop of beer and said he'd be going. Paddy mumbled to himself. Ron said absentmindedly that his brother-in-law used to sing beautiful. When they'd all gone, I tidied up the bottles and found that someone had nicked my soap dish. I tell you, there's not a lot of education about these days.

The Chairman

I GOT FRIENDLY WITH AN INDIAN ONCE," said the old-timer staring across the beer parlour at a swarthy young man playing pool. "A bit like that chap," he said, "only flashier. He wasn't from round these parts, though, he came from down south somewhere, said he was a semolina."

"Seminole," I murmured.

"Maybe," said the old-timer. "It was in the thirties, round about '35 I reckon; I was young then." He stared thoughtfully into his glass and I waved for a replacement. He was silent until it arrived.

"The Indian?" I prompted him.

"Well," he said, "he made history that Indian did—not the kind you study, all politics and wars and such, but history of a kind. He was a loner, to begin with. He didn't have no truck with the other Indians at all and they had no truck with him. He said they were a different lot, said he had different traditions and spoke different as well. He spoke well himself, had a deep kind of voice and a funny accent. I asked him about it once and he said he'd learned English from an Irishman. Paddy Indian we called him. Billy McMinn even said he looked a bit like his cousin from Kerry, which he might well have done. There's a lot of dark Irishmen about."

"Black celts," I said.

"Maybe so. Anyway, I was working as a builders' labourer then; a good few new houses were going up round about, and while they weren't very fancy they were better than the old log cabins, and it was fairly steady work. I was on the job one morning when Paddy Indian came by and started talking to me. That rather flattered me, you know. I mean he was older than me by a good bit, and, you know, he was sort of impressive, what with his long black hair and his way of talking. He said he'd been looking me over quite a while and he reckoned I was just the chap he'd been looking for. 'Looking for what?' I said. 'It's a secret,' he said. He said it so earnestly that I put my hammer down on a beam a bit carelessly and it fell on my foot. It wasn't a big hammer, but it was big enough. When I'd done hopping and cursing he said, 'Just as I thought. You've got the temperament.' 'What temperament?' I said, a bit crossly. He said, 'Behind the beer parlour at six.' They wouldn't let him into the beer parlour because he was an Indian, but I reckon he did all right.

"Well, we met where he said and he explained to me that these semolinas he belonged to had a way of seeing into the future, but it was a two-man job. He said the semolina chairman . . ."

"Shaman," I interjected.

". . . had to have a helper, a young man, an unmarried one, and that he'd picked me. 'What do I do?' I asked him. 'Well,' he said, 'we do a ritual, a sort of dance it is, and you ask me questions and I tell you what's going to happen. It's just little things at first,' he said, 'until we get practiced, and then we get the real stuff.' 'Like what?' I asked. 'Well,' he said, 'this is gold country isn't it?' 'You mean a strike?' 'Could be,' he said, 'could be. Of course being a chairman, I can't have any of it, but you could.' 'How much?' I said, being young and greedy. 'It depends,' he said. 'Might be a bit, might be a lot.' 'All right,' I said and he said, 'Shake,' and we shook hands; he had a funny sort of grip, not the usual at all. 'That's the bonding,' he told me. 'You're bonded.'

"I'd heard a bit about bondsmen from my Dad, and I knew it had something to do with money, though I wasn't very clear about it, but it sounded important, and when I got back home I was pretty excited. I was still living at home then, with my Mum and Dad, and it was all I could do to keep the secret, but I managed it, and the next night, about dusk, I met Paddy Indian again and we went up away from the town and he took me over to a dried-up creek that had been mined out, and he stood in the middle of the channel and started moaning. After a bit he said, 'It's coming through, but we have to paint you up a bit,' and he got some burned wood from his pocket and marked my face with it and drew circles on the back of my hands. Then he pulled out an eagle feather and said, 'Bite on that,' so I bit on it. I felt a bit daft with this feather sticking out of my mouth and even more so when he said, 'Now dance round me.' Well, I wasn't much of a dancer but I did my best, and he went on moaning and grunting. Then he said, 'Just for a start we'll try people. It's the easiest. Give me a name.' I gave him the first name which came into my head which was Jerry Wilkins, because he worked alongside me, and Paddy said, 'Nails.' He didn't say anything else, but he was standing there stiff as a post, looking expectant, so I guessed he wanted another name. I said, 'Janet McCallum,' because I was kind of sweet on her at the time. He said, 'Cat!' Janet didn't have a cat.

"It was a bit awkward talking with the feather in my mouth. It kept wobbling up and down, but I didn't dare take it out, though I was drooling a bit. I tried a third name. I said 'Hank Murray,' and he said 'Finding.' Then he sort of swayed a bit and said, 'That's enough. The spirit's leaving me. What did I say?' he asked me. Well, I told him and he said it wasn't much but it was a good start, and I had better wipe my hands and face and not to tell anyone. 'We'll have another crack at it in a couple of days,' he said.

"Well, I liked beer then just as I do now," he said with a meaningful stare, to which I responded appropriately. "The next night I was in the beer parlour with my Dad when Jerry Wilkins came in. He settled down with us, and said something funny had happened to him. He'd hung up his coat on a post, like he always does when he starts work, and when he put his hand in his pocket he found he'd got a pocketful of nails. I didn't say anything, but I had to bite my tongue pretty hard. Around then Janet's dad came in, and said that there had been a right going on at his place. They were just sitting down to supper when there was a great barking from the kitchen and he went to see what was up and the dog was making a fuss at a cat that had got in somehow and was sitting on top of the dresser looking a bit scared. Well Janet got it down—it was only a young thing—and comforted it, and it took to her. 'And so,' he said, 'I guess we have a cat now.' It was even harder keeping quiet this time, but I did it, and when I saw Hank across the room it was all I could do not to go across and ask him what had happened. I didn't need to ask, really. Things got around quick in those days and it wasn't very long before we heard that he'd found his dog that had gone missing that morning. It had just turned up, it seems, no worse for wear and not even hungry. Well, three times was too much. I had to tell someone or bust, so the next morning on the job I told Willie Black. Willie was really the last person I should have told, because he had about as much capacity to keep quiet as a man with his shirt tail on fire, so it got around pretty quickly.

"Things get exaggerated a bit when they circulate like that. I remember once I told a chap about my Dad having a gold filling and within a week or so there were people following him around all over the place because they thought he'd struck it rich. It got so that he couldn't go anywhere without someone watching him. Paddy Indian had the same experience. Folk were looking on him like some kind of prophet. One of them even went up to him outside the beer parlour and asked him if he'd like a drink brought out, and what did he think of the boxing match they'd got going on Sunday between the big Dutchman and the Welsh miner. He said 'The dark will go down,' and sure enough, the black-headed Welshman went down, though some said that the Dutchman would have done just as well, him wearing black shorts.

"I was keen for another dance in the dried up creek channel but Paddy kept putting me off. He said the moon had to be at the full and he had to have a red handkerchief. I didn't know what the red handkerchief was for, but my Dad had one and I borrowed it, and when we got to the place and he'd marked me with the burnt wood and stuck the feather in my mouth he tied it round his eyes and said, 'The eyes of the spirit need the darkness,' which made me wonder why he'd picked a moonlit night. Well, it all went on as before, only this time he said to ask him something different. He said just to ask him what he saw. I said, 'What do you see?' and he grunted and moaned a bit and said he saw a death. I pretty near lost my feather but I managed to grab it before it fell, and I had the sense to ask him, 'Who?' He did a lot of groaning after that and then he said he saw a young woman in black, a yellow-headed woman, he added. Then he gave a sort of gulp and bent a bit as if he'd been winded, and took the handkerchief off. 'I can't go on,' he said. 'I feel as if I've been hit by something. What did I tell you?' 'A death,' I told him, 'and something about a yellow-headed girl in black.' 'Ah, it's a desperate thing the second sight,' he said. 'The second sight is what we semolinas call it—it's like the first sight only it comes afterwards when you've got the red blindfold on by the full moon,' he explained. I nodded as wisely as I could. 'We'll do it again in a few days,' he said. 'It was too strong. You're only young; you're not up to the full dose.' I wasn't quite clear what I had got to do with it, but he explained that if I'd been a bit more practiced he wouldn't have had to stop like that. 'You'd have kept the bad stuff off,' he said. 'I'd have seen the good things. We'll have to have another crack.'

"There was no way I could keep this to myself, and everywhere I went I was looking at yellow-headed women, and feeling sorry for them, and after a couple of days so was everyone else. I was a bit famous myself by this time, as everyone knew I was the chairman's assistant. My Dad said I was stupid to get mixed up with Indians but he wasn't mad about it. He said that there might be something in it. Indians, he said, were kind of strange; he'd known one down country that could trap better than anyone he'd ever met and had a medicine that cured all sorts of things. Anyway, as I said, I was quite famous and people kept coming up to me and asking when the death was going to happen, and when were we going to do our stuff again. The yellow-headed women were the most upset, and there were a good few about. Minnie McFarlane asked me if women that made their hair yellow counted. I said I guessed it was the colour that did it, not where the colour came from. One woman dyed her hair back to brown again but her best friend told her it was too late, and she didn't have a best friend after that.

"It wasn't Minnie McFarlane that fulfilled the prophecy though, it was Angel Sweet. I don't think her real name was either Angel or Sweet, but she got one name for looking angelic, which she wasn't, and the other for being sweet on men, which she was. Anyway, a couple of days after the word got around, there was Angel walking down the street in black and mopping her eyes with a handkerchief, and telling everyone her uncle had died in Vancouver. The woman in the post office said there had been no telegram or even a letter for her, come to that, but Angel said it had been a personal message brought up by a friend of her uncle who'd just dropped in to tell her and now he'd gone back.

"All through this Paddy Indian kept himself to himself. He looked, well, aloof is how you'd put it, I guess. He didn't talk much, he never did, but now he grunted more often than spoke. He had been working in a sawmill up 'til then, and he still went on working, but didn't get much done because everyone kept interrupting him. It was enough to drive a man crazy, but he only lost his temper once when, after Bill Halpern had asked him to keep the rain off on Saturday when there was a picnic, he said 'I don't do rain,' and stamped his foot rather hard and hit a sharpish stone.

"It was Wednesday when Paddy Indian called me back to my duties as assistant chairman. He said we needn't go to the creek this time, there was no need. We'd just go to a little gully a bit off the road out of town. 'No-one will know,' he said. He told me that outside the beer parlour on Tuesday night. He had three or four glasses lined up beside him, and he spoke more loudly than I thought he should. I said, 'Ssssh,' but he didn't pay any attention, and I can't be sure exactly who it was coming back from the outhouse just then and well within earshot, but I think it was Willie Black.

"Anyway, we got to the gully just as the moon was coming up and this time he'd put on a bangle that rattled and had drawn a couple of red lines on his face. He was a bit louder too, and when he started to groan and I began to dance around him it was bright enough for me to see a couple of white patches on the lip of the gully. I said, in a whisper, 'We're being watched,' but I reckon he didn't hear me. He went stiff as a post like before and I knew it was time for the questions. He said 'What do I see?' which was my line and I got a bit confused and said, 'Well, what, then?' and he spun around a bit—he'd never done that before, and said, 'It's the spirit right enough. Would you ever ask me the question?' Well I asked him and he did a great groan and said, 'I see a feast.' Well, that was easy. I said, 'The town picnic, you mean?' He gave another hefty groan and said, 'Those that go to the feast will have great fortune if they bless the spirits.' 'What do you mean, bless the spirits?' I asked him. He gave a grunt or two. 'Those that go to the feast and leave nothing under their pillows will find nothing; those that leave paper will find paper, those that leave gold . . .' and he began to sort of stutter. 'What is it?' I asked him. He sort of gasped and said, 'It's too powerful. It's gold spirit. The spirit is burning me up.' And he clutched at his middle. He was bent almost double, and he said very quiet. 'There will be a sign,' he shouted, stretching up straight again, and pointing his face up at the sky. 'What sign?' I asked, my feather wobbling; I was getting pretty excited. 'Grief is over; joy is here!' he said and sort of keeled over.

"I dropped the feather and stuffed it in my pocket and helped him to his feet. He was quite heavy and it was a bit of a struggle. 'What did I tell you?' he said, and I told him just as I've told you and he said, 'Well then, you'd better go to the picnic and make your fortune. Of course, I can't go. The chairman mustn't benefit from his prophecies. Devil a bit of it can he get,' and he gave a huge sigh. 'Then why do you do it?' I asked him as we got back to the road. 'Sure, it comes over me,' he said. 'It's my calling. It's what a chairman has to do!' 'What sort of sign do you think it'll be?' I asked him. 'How will we know?' He turned to me. 'We?' he said. 'Isn't it a secret between the two of us?' Well, I could hardly believe he thought that, particularly as we could both hear an excited chattering going on ahead of us on the road back to town, so I just said, 'Of course it is,' though I went on wondering about the sign.

"Practically everybody was wondering about that sign. One chap thought he'd seen it when he saw a flickering light in his yard the next night, and he rushed outside, but it was only Tom Winston, who'd been in his outhouse because he'd got caught short and was lighting his pipe. Another fellow had a dream about lobsters, but nobody thought that meant much as he'd come from Newfoundland. Besides, we couldn't see what that had to do with grief being over and joy being here, unless you were particularly fond of lobsters. Minnie McFarlane had the best one; her husband left her, and while we all agreed that she'd lost a lot of grief it didn't seem quite right somehow.

"It was the day before the picnic that the sign came and there was no mistaking it. Angel Sweet ran into the post store and told everyone that her uncle hadn't died at all, it had been a mistake, and that he had sent her a present up the road. She'd just had a message. It was her rich uncle, she said, and waved her hand around, flapping it so that everyone could see the big glittery ring she'd got. 'It's the sign,' someone said, and Angel said, 'What sign?' and they told her and she said it was all stupid and had nothing to do with any prophecies and she wasn't going to the picnic anyway and she had better things to do. Someone said, 'A bit more joy?' and someone else said, 'Who is he?' but she flounced out, and Simon Grant said God makes use of strange instruments, though none of us were too sure that Paddy's spirits had much to do with God.

"I dare say you're well ahead of me by this time, and you're right. People never locked their doors in those days, so when we all got back from the town picnic there wasn't anything left under the pillows, and a few other things had gone as well, and neither Paddy Indian nor Angel Sweet were anywhere to be found.

"Well, those that had believed in him and put stuff under their pillows were very sore about it, but they didn't like to let on, and a couple of fellows had trouble with their wives. Me, I didn't have any trouble to speak of. I'd seen what Paddy had made his red marks on his face with, and I'd guessed where he'd borrowed the lipstick, and Angel Sweet had always been good with cats. I had the sense to tell Willie Black, in confidence, that I'd lost my savings, and he believed I had some, and so I wasn't blamed too much.

"Telling makes you dry," the old-timer said.

I attended to the problem, and when the beer had arrived I asked him, "But what about making history?"

He took a good pull at his beer. "Well," he said, "I hear tell they call it channelling now, and it must have been about the first time anyone did any channelling in Cariboo. Besides that," he said, "when I picked Paddy Indian up there in the gully, I saw something. It must be the first time that any Indian, Semolina or otherwise, had a shamrock tattooed on his left elbow."

The Loose Connection

I DON'T KNOW WHO YOU ARE. You may be my Aunt Edna, for all I can tell, or a librarian in Indiana, or even a con in Alcatraz. You might be anybody, but of course you're not. You're somebody. You're a person with your own time and place. You are you, quite definitely you. Do hang on to that conviction. It's important that you do. If you don't, well, you can find yourself becoming very confused indeed. As I did, as I am, in fact. Maybe you can tell this already. I kind of hope so. If you don't understand that I'm confused you won't understand anything, or at least you won't understand much.

I wasn't going to tell you—whoever you are—about all this at first. I thought I'd better keep it dark. Besides, I couldn't remember some of it. I only recollected the highlights: the paintings of women, the man's portrait over the mantelpiece, and the time the mirror appeared, and of course I couldn't forget the house itself. I'll never forget that house. Still, I wouldn't have been able to sort it all out at all if it hadn't been for the diary. That was one of the things I'd forgotten, but when I discovered it at the bottom of a pile of junk in the basement it all came back to me, and some things that weren't in the diary at all.

Maybe I should start there, with the diary I mean. It introduces itself fairly efficiently, so I don't need to explain it, or describe it. The first day is October 12, 1967. I hope you like reading diaries. I don't much myself. As someone once wrote, Samuel Pepys gives me the crepys. Very witty, really. I wonder how he would have rhymed Evelyn or Parson Woodforde. But I'm delaying, as you can see; I'm putting it off. Well, it's not surprising. It's a bit difficult to tell anyone, even you, who are so much a somebody, so much your own person. You are, aren't you? I certainly am these days. Or I think I am. But there was a time when I became someone else's person. At least that's one way of putting it. Anyway, here's the diary.

October 12, 1967: Dear diary—isn't that the way one is supposed to begin? I seem to remember that from somewhere. Dear Diary, I do not really know why I am beginning you, but you are such a handsome book that I have to write something on your blank pages and after all today is a new beginning. Do I need to explain? I suppose so. All right, then, Dear Diary, I am writing this in an old house on Fitzwalter Street which I have rented for the winter academic term. Professor Arnold Gold, who owns it, has gone away until the spring to France and Italy I rather believe—and he offered it to the University for temporary teachers, and I am one of those. It's odd explaining this to you. I feel somehow as if you should know this already. After all, I'm your owner, am I not? But it seems necessary. The house has been looked after most carefully, and restored somewhat to its original splendour. It's not a mansion exactly, but it is big, and built around 1910, very solid, tall ceilings, some late art nouveau glass, wood panelling—a bit dark to my taste—and so forth. I don't need to say any more, do I? Good. Well, here I am, and really very comfortable. It is a bit odd to be the sole inhabitant, but apparently the University couldn't find a married couple or a family for this period, so that was that, and the rent is terribly reasonable. Unreasonable almost. Two hundred a month. Fantastic actually.

I am not sure what else to tell you. I've not kept a diary before. I suppose the day's events are appropriate, but what's so new about giving classes on art history? No, this is not going to be a record of that part of my life. Unfortunately for you, dear diary, there isn't another part. Not yet, at any rate. I only moved in today. I haven't met the neighbours. I'm not sure one does meet neighbours any more. Good fences between the houses may be the reason. The fence around this one is about ten foot. And there's a huge hedge out front. I'm not overlooked, that's for sure. Not outside the garden at any rate. In the house though, I am, or feel as if I am. By the house itself, or perhaps what is in the house. I feel watched. It's just being in a new place, I suppose. And all that dark panelling. So much for that. I've started, Dear Diary, so don't feel too disappointed. Tomorrow I'll do better.

October 13, 1967: Dear Diary, I've settled in quite well now. I'm not as lonely as I thought I'd be. I've got my books alongside the owner's in the small den on the ground floor, and that's where I'm writing this, by the light of a lamp that looks as if it might be Tiffany. The living room is where I mean to relax, read and so forth. Though when I was in there earlier the standard lamp flickered often enough to be irritating. Probably a loose connection, but it made reading a little tiresome. I must get someone in to look at it. I must get a TV too. There isn't one. Surprising, really. There isn't a radio either. Well, maybe I'll get more work done that way. The room itself is almost imposing, largely because of the pictures. There's a fine oil above the mantelpiece, a portrait of a man. Nineteenth century, clearly. Pupil of Raeburn? Or could be a copy. And there are five other oils of women, about the same period, and a little landscape. Could almost be a Constable. It's the Raeburn that dominates the room though, but there's something about it that bothers me. Maybe he's the reason I came here into the den, as much as the flickering lamp. It's late. I'm getting fanciful. And So To Bed. Isn't that the right phrase?

October 14: Something odd about this house, Dear Diary. I have to tell you this before the rest of the stuff. It's the living room—drawing room maybe I should say—it's dark, but not just physically dark. It's dark in itself. It has its own darkness. Am I making myself clear? I guess not. And in the evening that painting gets brighter as the room gets darker. I don't mean phosphorescent or anything like that. I mean like it's been—or is being—restored. Remember how Velasquez brightened when they cleaned him up? Silly of me. How can a diary remember that? Still, that's the way it is. Brighter. And a couple of other pictures look brighter, too. I really must get a TV.

Nothing much on the work front. Thirty-two students, all fairly average, except for one. Ellen Byrne her name is. Attractive. Older than the rest. Around late twenties I'd say. Red hair. And a touch of Irish brogue in her speech. Otherwise the classes are as usual. I can't get too excited about them, even for you, Diary dear.

October 15: The electrician says there's nothing wrong with the standard lamp, or the plugs and wiring anywhere in the room. He came round mid-afternoon, and everything worked perfectly. But this evening the lights flickered again, the chandelier as well as the standard lamp. I told myself maybe it was a local overload, though I don't know much about these things. Or maybe it's the cool of the evening makes the metal contract or something so the connections become loose. Is that possible? I don't know. But I do know that there's something very odd about the room. The pictures are changing. I'm sure of it. They're all growing brighter and the room darker. I don't want to think about it.

A boring visiting lecturer today. John Singer Sargent As Caricaturist. Dull, dull, dull. Some of my students were there, including Ellen Byrne, so I took her for a drink afterwards. She's a mature student, after all. Twenty-eight. I looked her up in the Department records. So I wasn't out of line.

October 18: I missed out, Dear Diary. Sorry about that. But that's the way diaries are. Went on a weekend trip with Ellen. Don't make that face at me. (Do diaries make faces? Well, I felt you did.) We drove out to see the Gutenhaus Collection in that big mansion the old man turned into his personal museum in the woods. Great scenery, and some interesting stuff. Ellen was fascinated, and it was dark before we left the place so we didn't drive back but put up at a little motel. All very—or almost very—proper. We had separate rooms, anyway. Returning here though, the room is darker than before, and the paintings brighter still. The crypto-Raeburn is—well, it's past brightening—it's almost begun to be washed out. I mean, the highlights are brighter too. But it's the Raeburn that's the leader. Why did I say 'Leader?' Do you know, Diary? I don't. To bed, anyway.

October 19: The opthalmologist—how the hell do you spell that?—says there's nothing wrong with my eyes, and I'm not suffering from nervous tension. Maybe so, but there's something wrong about what they see—when I'm in the house, at any rate. Raeburn has a sort of sheen on him—or it—no matter where I stand he—it—reflects light. Even when there isn't much. The other paintings—well, they're bright but not like it—him. Funny selection really. All early nineteenth century I'd say. Apart from the Raeburn gentleman—oh very much the gentleman in that formal dress, there are five ladies—Did I tell you?—and a little wee landscape. I rather like the landscape. It doesn't look superior, as do all the women. There's a family resemblance, too, or a sort of resemblance. Maybe it's just the same painter. Or perhaps they were Raeburn's sisters, or daughters. Or mistresses?

Asked Ellen out to dinner tomorrow. Otherwise not much to tell.

October 21: Took Ellen to dinner last night. She asked where I was living. I told her and she said it was a house she'd always been curious about, so after dinner I brought her back here. Funny thing. She said, "Not here. Not in this room," and so I said, "Where then?" And she said, "Where do you sleep?" So I took her upstairs and she stayed the night. In point of fact we overslept and it was a rush to get away in the morning. Not even time for coffee. Damn these 8:30 lectures! But, leaving, I remembered my box of slides was in the living room and I dashed in and grabbed it off the occasional table. The Raeburn caught my eye as I practically ran out, and all I saw was a silvery glaze—like glass. Odd that. After all, being an oil, it wasn't glazed. When I got back I came straight here—to my study—I haven't been in the living room again. I don't want to. But I feel drawn to it. Still, I mustn't. I don't know why I mustn't, but I really mustn't. To bed, to bed, to bed.

October 23: After classes took Ellen for a drink. She asked me about The Room. She said it with capitals. I had nothing to tell her. She said it felt funny, as if she were being watched. She took a deep breath. She said, "When you put your hand in my blouse I . . . even thought I heard something." I laughed. I said, "The voice of conscience?" "No," she said, "no." She was quite serious. We went on to dinner. She has an apartment in Carter Street, so afterwards we went there. When I got back here I went into the living room. I shouldn't have done that. It wasn't whispers, it was giggles. Little thin giggles. I have to admit, Dear Diary, that I fled.

October 24: It was much worse this evening. The room was darker than ever, and the paintings at their brightest. I must get a TV. Nothing else to say. I'm too tired. Much too tired. Ellen has a headache. She said it was a headache. I have one, in any case. No more now.

October 25: Got a TV. It didn't work. It just flickered and then went dead. I took it into this study and it worked fine. But not in the living room. One of the four bulbs in the living room chandelier has failed, too. I must replace it. Ellen doesn't fancy coming to the house any more and she has a visitor at her apartment, a girlfriend from the east.

October 26: Late back from work because of a stupid meeting. It was dusk outside. Only dusk. But the living room was pitch black. Turned on the chandelier light and all the bulbs had gone. But the paintings were visible somehow. Shining in a way. Especially Raeburn. It was like a mirror. I almost went up to it but something held me back.

Ellen is looking up the history of the house; she says something is very wrong. Her visitor hasn't left yet.

October 27: After dinner with Ellen I came back here. It may have been the wine gave me courage, but I went into the living room. No lights of course. And I went up to the Raeburn. It shone like glass, like a mirror. I looked into it. It was me. There I was in nineteenth century costume, in a mirror. And I heard more giggling. I had the courage of the wine, I suppose. I said, right out loud, "What the hell are you playing at, whoever—whatever— you are?" There was no reply. I left, walking as slowly as I could manage. By the door I flicked the light switch just once for the hell of it, and all the bulbs lit up. Then they went out again. "Loose connection," I said loudly. I felt as if I were insulting the room. I intended to. "Just a loose connection," I said again, and I shrugged. That was all. Bed, Bed, Bed. I find these days really exhausting.

October 28: Ellen has left with her visitor for a long weekend. A very long one as far as I'm concerned. The TV works fine in my study. Watched an old movie and started on the students' essays. Read Ellen's first and found a sort of postscript: "I asked around about the house and Arnold Gold and the pictures. He took the house in 1960 and the paintings arrived this last summer. I know about that because he showed them off to his colleagues." "Why didn't you ask them about it?" I said, aloud, and then, stupidly, "I didn't like to!" The note continued: "It seems he got them from England, and that the man is an ancestor of some kind, a painter, and the portrait is a self-portrait. The women, Gold said, were some of his subjects. He was a bachelor and had no children. There was a family rumour about the one in the red, some sort of titled lady, but Gold put no reliance on it. Funny thing, though. After that one little gathering to show off the pictures, Gold didn't invite anyone over, not even for drinks, and he changed his plan to leave his wife and kids behind when he went off on sabbatical. He took them with him."

She stopped there. I felt an urge to go into the living room, but I didn't. That room is too much for me. Maybe it was too much for Gold. Should I lock it up?

October 29: Went into the living room this evening. My mistake. The lights didn't work. The Raeburn was a mirror again. I looked into it. The reflection was me—was mine, and I was once more wearing his clothes—the portrait's clothes that is, and when I turned round—I don't know how to put this—the women, first one, then the others, one by one, as I went round the room were—or looked like—eggs. Yes, eggs. I don't mean they were egg shaped, just that those oval faces had no noses, no eyes, no mouths. Anaconic they were. I staggered a bit. I said, "Hallucination," out loud, then I bent and looked at the little landscape. And the landscape was different, too. It had been a little meadow and a brook with a hill in the background and a copse on the left, but it wasn't that at all now. It was another place. It was a place I'd never seen before.

I went to bed in a daze, but I kept my head. It was a controlled hallucination. I mean, I knew I was hallucinating. Part of me stayed quite detached. I slept well.

October 30: Ellen phoned me this evening. She's back in town. She said did I read her stuff? I told her she'd got an A. She said she meant the other stuff, about the house and the paintings. I said, "Yes." She said, "Do you suppose those women were his mistresses then?" I said whatever they had been, they were now eggs. I had to explain that.

"And the landscape," I said. "The landscape what?" she asked. I said, "Look. I know you hate the place, but come round tomorrow and let's look at it all together." "All right," she said. "And stay the night," I said. She said, "We'll see." That's all that's worth putting down. Except that she really did deserve the A. It was on Samuel Prout, and she'd caught his mood exactly. I've always enjoyed Prout.

November 1: Ellen came round last night at about eight. It was dark outside, but the living room seemed even darker and the lights didn't work. I said, "Look at the Raeburn." She said, "I can't see a thing. It's too dark." I had an inspiration. I said, "Close your eyes," and led her in front of the Raeburn. "Now keep tight hold of my hand and open your eyes and look!" She gave a little gasp. "It's you," she said. "It's a mirror," I said. She said, "No. It's you. It isn't me." "Look at the women," I said, and led her to them, still holding her hand. "They're eggs, aren't they?" I said, almost triumphantly. "No," she said, "they're not—they're . . . well, they're . . . It's a trick," she said helplessly. "It's like one-way mirrors. It's something to do with the glass." "They're not glazed," I pointed out. "But they reflect," she said . . . "I can see myself in every one of them, a bit blurred," and then she said, "Oh!" "Oh, what?" I asked her. "The red one," she said. "It's not blurred at all. It's me." She was clinging to my arm now, not only to my hand.

"What about the landscape?" I asked, and as she bent to look at it she let my hand go. "Trees, meadow, stream, hill," she said. I took her hand again. "Ohhhh," she said, "Ohhh," and then, "I think I understand." I looked into her face. The room seemed less dark now, and I could see her eyes shining. She let go my hand and sat on the couch. "I won't ask you to take me to the bedroom this time," she said.

We moved up to the bedroom at around three, and when we came down in the morning the room wasn't dark anymore, or didn't feel dark, which is the same thing, I suppose. The paintings were as they had been when I first saw them. Ellen said, "I think it's over." She went to the little landscape and bent and looked at it. "The lights work," I said. "It must have been a loose connection." "Yes," she said, and gave a funny giggle. Then she went over and looked at the landscape. "It's back to normal," she said. "It was nothing much—a pretty little piece really—do you remember my essay?" "Yes," I said. "Well," she said, "it wasn't this kind of Constableish thing—it wasn't a landscape at all—it was a street scene with two people in the foreground—I knew it immediately—it was a Samuel Prout."

"But you wrote your essay . . ." I said. "Yes," she said, and then, "I think maybe after all those models—or mistresses—especially the one in the red—he wanted something different." "Something different?" I asked. She smiled. "The same but different," she said. "And, do you know, I have a funny feeling inside me that maybe . . . maybe we've given him it." "What?" I said. She said, "If I have a baby because of you, I will call him Raeburn—or maybe Crypto-Raeburn. Would you like a son called Crypto-Raeburn Rogers? I've got to rush or I'll miss class." And she was gone.

I'm writing this, Dear Diary, at five o'clock, and I'm writing it in the living room. The room is quite bright, really, with the sharp light of the end of fall, and the portraits are only portraits. I wonder if I will marry Ellen. And I wonder if she will have a baby. And I wonder, too—but there's her ring at the door. Tomorrow, Dear Diary, I'll tell you more.

I didn't tell the diary more. It stops there. I can tell you, though. We did get married a couple of months later, and it wasn't just because of the baby. We didn't call him Crypto Raeburn, though we called him Samuel Raeburn Rogers. Ellen insisted on Samuel because of Samuel Prout, and also because she swears he was conceived on Halloween, which the Irish call Samhain though they pronounce it quite differently from how it looks. I suppose that was reasonable. They do say, too, that the dead return on Halloween, and considering the way that portrait changed I suppose there may be a loose connection.

Odd

"IT'S REALLY TERRIBLY ODD," he said, leaning forward in his chair, a little intensely.

She smiled gently. "Don't you mean *they're* odd?" she enquired and he followed the direction of her glance, and noticed his socks. "One blue, one brown."

"Yes," he said and sighed a little. "It's not even as if I were colour blind," he mourned, "though I suppose I could pretend I was, if anyone noticed."

"*I* noticed," she said, "and so would anyone else. And, if you don't mind my mentioning it, your shirt is misbuttoned. Do I make you nervous, or something? I mean, is that it?"

"Not at all," he said, rather too forcefully to be complimentary. "Not a bit of it."

"Well," she said, adjusting her skirt downwards over her knees, and with a slight edge in her voice, "what has got into you, then? You've forgotten to trim your beard on one side, too. Don't you ever look in a mirror?"

He stood up and took a couple of restless paces. "That's what I wanted to talk to you about. I have to talk to somebody about it."

"And I got elected, eh?"

"Yes. You're so . . . understanding."

"When a man tells a girl she's understanding it usually means he does not find her attractive," she commented.

"I don't mean that at all," he said hurriedly, "not at all. You *are* attractive. Very attractive. And I'm attracted. But . . ."

"But what?"

He sat down again suddenly. "Look into my eyes," he commanded. "What do you see?"

She brushed the long hair away from her brow and peered intensely. "I don't see any love-light, that's for sure," she said, "and they aren't more than predictably bloodshot. What am I supposed to see?"

"Look harder," he said. "Pretend they are two marbles. Compare."

"I see what you mean. I noticed it before. They're not quite the same colour, are they? They don't match!"

He leaned back in the chair. "They're odd. Odd is the word. And the whole thing is odd."

"I think we have reached the point where I forget that you invited me round for a drink with all the conventional implications, and put on my mother's help expression and say 'tell me all about it,'" she said, not without a touch of bitterness. "But maybe I could—do you think—have that drink anyway? I suspect this is going to be a long story."

He jumped to his feet. "I'm so sorry, but I'm flustered. I'm forgetting myself. Gin? Scotch? What?"

"I think a Scotch," she said, "and make it a double. Have one yourself," she added kindly. "It may ease things a little."

As he went into the tiny kitchen she glanced round the living room. Her eye moved casually over the pictures and she sighed. A Mondrian with its geometrical precision neatly confined by a soberly thin frame, a mathematically precise Ben Nicholson poster, a small angular Paul Klee. On the mantelpiece was a Rubik's cube. "Square," she muttered, then noticed a smaller picture. She got up to look at it. It was a reproduction of a Landseer spaniel, all glossy warmth and liquid eyes. "Odd," she murmured, smiling, and then, looking around further she saw that the record rack by the stereo was filled with magazines. As he returned and handed her the Scotch she asked him curiously, "Where do you keep your L.P.s?"

"In a cupboard." She raised her elegant eyebrows a little. "Yes," he said, "It *is* odd," and he shuddered before taking a sip of his drink.

"Now I am really curious," she told him. "Your socks are odd; your eyes are odd; and your apartment is . . . well . . . rather oddly organized. What exactly is happening?"

"I wish I knew. It began about ten days ago, just after we met—at Barbara Seffins' party—remember?"

"I remember," she said. "You told me I was the most attractive girl in the room."

"Yes. And you were," he added with undue emphasis, "you surely were."

"But now I have dwindled into being a confidante," she murmured, and made a little moue.

"Not dwindled," he said, "truly, not dwindled—can't you understand? I need you!"

"In what way exactly?"

He bit his lip. "I need to tell you things, I need you to tell me what I should do—if there's anything I can do."

"I heard that drink was aphrodisiac," she said thoughfully, "but isn't it working a little rapidly? And don't you know what to do?"

"Not that!" he said. "I mean, not now, not yet at any rate."

"Later perhaps?"

He sat down again. "Listen, damn you. Listen to me, and stop teasing!"

She sighed. "All right, spill it!"

"It happened, as I said, just after we first met," he told her. "I was invited to a Saturday night dinner at a really very stylish restaurant. It was my boss's golden wedding anniversary and a chap in the office organized it. I asked him about dress and what was expected of the guests. I believe one should always behave in accordance with people's expectations."

"Tonight being an exception."

"Yes, well," he said, "I gathered it was black tie and I was . . . expected . . . required to wear a buttonhole as it was a festive occasion. I was told there would be the usual toasts. It was all, you might say, predictable, and I went along there with no qualms at all. I really enjoy these occasions. Neatness, formality, order— these things give life a kind of dignity, I've always felt."

The girl shuddered. "Do you mind if I smoke?"

"Of course not," he said, "I'll get you an ashtray," and he reached under his chair and produced a piece of misshapen pottery with a dent in one side to indicate its function. She looked at it wonderingly. "I bought it last week," he said miserably, "at a flea market."

"I hadn't supposed you got it at Sotheby's."

"It is appalling," he admitted, "but that's the way everything has been since that night."

The girl's frown of puzzlement cleared, and she said with the air of one who had at last seen the light, "You had a seizure, didn't you? You had a fit of some kind. That's it! You became temporarily deranged!"

He groaned a little. "Deranged possibly," he said, "and I pray temporarily, but it doesn't feel like it—I just can't stop."

"Can't stop what?"

"Well, behaving oddly—acting out of character. Ever since that night."

"What precisely happened that night?" she enquired. "How did Jekyll become Hyde? Was it the soup?"

"It was the manager," he said. "At least, I think he was the manager. He came over from the general office area and spoke to the Maitre d' and the Wine Steward, and then he asked the boss if everything was to his satisfaction and, well, I wasn't the only one who noticed it." He paused.

"Noticed what?" said the girl, stubbing out her cigarette impatiently, and lifting her glass and contemplating the ice.

"You've finished your drink," he said. "Would you care for another?"

"First tell me what you noticed," she said, "and then get me a drink. The revelation may put me into shock."

He looked at her dubiously. There had been a trace of acid in her voice. "I noticed," he said slowly, "that his socks were odd. One was white and one black."

"Ohh."

"Yes, and everyone else noticed it too."

"Ah," she said, "and you were collectively stunned?" She held up her glass. He ignored it.

"It wasn't only that," he said, "it was his eyes too."

"One was black and the other white?" enquired the girl with the air of one eager to please. She rattled the ice in her glass.

"No, it was just that one of them sort of wandered off to one side—I mean it looked away—a wall-eye I think they call it."

"So?" said the girl. She lifted her glass to her lips and sipped delicately at the ice water.

He noticed her action. "I'll get you another."

"Thank you." She smiled brightly. "This is a truly fascinating story."

He returned with the glass and sat down again. "Does it go on much longer?" she enquired. "It's not that I didn't bring my tooth-brush. I did. But I can only handle so much Scotch at a sitting."

"Look, I'm sorry. But I'll try to keep it brief. It wasn't my fault at all. It was Harbison. He fancies himself a humourist. He had no sooner noticed the wall-eye than he sang softly, 'What do you say to the One-eyed Riley' in his version of an Irish accent. I cannot believe that anyone heard it other than myself and a couple of others, but it was so apposite that it tickled my funny-bone. It may have been the wine. I'm not really used to drinking."

"So I noticed," murmured the girl.

He paid no attention. "Anyway, I laughed out loud, and sud-denly I saw the wall-eye fixed on me. It positively pinned me to my chair. It looked malevolent somehow—and I couldn't help re-membering all that stuff about the evil eye—the *mal occhio*—it's nonsense of course—but every country seems to have a word for it—the Spanish call it the *mal de ojo*, and the French the *mauvais oeil*. There are words for it in Armenian, Arabic, Greek, even Copt. The Copts call it *Bon*."

"Will there be a test at the end of the course?"

"I'm sorry," he said, "but I went into the subject a bit afterwards. I mean, after it all started happening. I am sure it was the eye." He shuddered a little.

The girl took a deep breath. "What started happening, exactly?" she enquired. "Let's have some action, shall we? Of at least some kind," she added.

"I couldn't forget it," he said, "the eye, I mean. It kept coming back to me. And that night when I went to bed it was positively haunting me. And then—well I should explain that I have poor circulation and so I wear bedsocks as well as pyjamas, but that night when I got into bed I discovered that I not only hadn't put on my socks, I hadn't put on my pyjamas either. I was quite naked. It was very strange. I never go to bed in the nude."

The girl looked at him quizzically. "I believe you," she said, "God knows, I believe you!"

"That was only the beginning," he said. "The next morning I put on odd socks. Deliberately. I couldn't help myself. It was a compulsion. There were several pairs in the drawer, all neatly organized, and I took out two pairs and selected a sock from each one and put them on. Can you believe it?"

"I once put on a man's Y fronts by mistake one morning," she said. "He laughed like anything!"

"That's not the same thing," he said. "I mean I wasn't absent-minded. It was a deliberate choice. I wanted to do this crazy thing, but it didn't seem crazy at the time. It seemed entirely sensible."

"I know what you mean. This very evening I had something crazy in mind—'til this moment I didn't know just how crazy."

He did not look at her. He stared into the distance. "Then," he said, "it all began. I never wear a buttonhole normally, but the next morning on the way to church . . ."

The girl leaned forward. "Excuse me," she said, "but did you say church?"

"Yes," he said, "on the way to church . . ."

"I thought so," she said.

"Well, on the way I saw a florist's open and I felt I had to have a buttonhole, and I went in and I bought a daffodil."

The girl sat up. "A daffodil?"

"Yes," he said, "and I put it in my buttonhole, and when the collection plate came round I . . . well, I . . . gave them the daffodil." The girl giggled. "It wasn't funny," he said, "it was embarrassing."

"Yes," she said, "I see that, I see that. Embarrassing, yes. And in church. It would be," and she gave a little snort of laughter.

"Don't laugh," he said, "that was just the beginning."

The girl leaned forward and picked up her glass and took a hefty gulp. "This is becoming fun," she said, "not quite the fun I antici-pated, but fun anyway. Do go on."

He gave her a dubious look. "After church, I came home and put a magazine on the record player."

She covered her pretty mouth with her hand to stifle her giggle. "You what?"

"I put a magazine on the record player. It was a copy of *The Smithsonian*."

"Yes," she said, "it would be. Or *The Economist*."

"I even put the needle on."

"Did it play?"

He frowned at her. "No. Of course not," he said. "I mean how could it?"

"Perhaps *God Bless America*—just a bar or two," she suggested, "or the *Alleluia Chorus*."

"Be serious!" he told her. "It really wasn't funny at all. Of course I took the thing away, and then I put the records in the cupboard and the magazine in the record rack and decided I needed a drink to settle my nerves."

"Me, too," she said, holding out her glass.

He ignored it. "I put cocoa in the teapot," he told her, "and then I, well, I just gave up. I was exhausted. So I put on my overcoat and went to bed!" The girl could not help it. She laughed out loud. He stood up.

"I thought you'd be sympathetic."

"Oh, I am," she assured him. "I truly am. I'm a very sympathetic person. But . . ." and she relapsed into giggles.

He gave a tentative smile. "I suppose it is funny, really. I mean, to someone else. But not to me."

"I'm sorry. I'll try to behave. Do go on!"

"All right," he said. "Well, things went from bad to worse. I went to work on Monday wearing a tie I picked up from the garbage can by the back gate door. It was hanging out over the edge of the can and I saw it and picked it up and put it on. It was horrible. It had a naked woman on it. It was worse than the daffodil."

"Much worse," she said, her face stiff with solemnity, but the muscles at the points of her jaw twitched, and her breasts were gently heaving.

"The boss didn't like it. He told me that he supposed it was a joke, but not a very good one. He told me to take it off, but I couldn't untie it. My fingers and thumbs wouldn't work. I had to borrow a pair of nail scissors from a typist and cut it off."

The girl said, "If there's any more of this I think I should have another drink. Don't worry, I'll get it myself."

"All right," he said. "You'll find the whisky in the oven."

She made it to the kitchen without laughing, but once there she leaned on the counter and gave way to silent hysteria. Her hand shook as she poured the whisky. "Oh God!" She took a stiff pull, drew a couple of deep breaths, topped up the glass and returned to the living room. He was putting on his raincoat. "Are you going out?" she asked, surprised.

"No," he said, "I just felt . . . er . . . cold. I just felt I had to put on my raincoat."

"Fine," she said. "It takes all sorts. Some men I know are devoted to raincoats." She collapsed into the chair and dabbed her eyes with a handkerchief.

He sat on the floor, cross-legged, and said, "Now you understand, don't you? I'm hexed. It's the evil eye. It's the *Mal Occhio*."

"The *Bon*," she agreed. "It's the good old *Bon*. As in Bonkers." Her voice was a little slurred.

He looked at her narrowly. "Aren't you drinking rather a lot?"

"Yesh—or rather yes," she said, "but what else can a girl do? Don't answer that. You'd get the answer wrong anyway." She put her hand to her mouth to soften the burp.

"But what can I do?" he said. "I mean, am I really truly crazy or what?"

"We're both crazy. I was crazy to come here and you were crazy to invite me."

"But I thought . . . I thought—I mean you were so . . . when we . . . I thought we were friends."

"Friends," she said thoughtfully. "Yes, friends. Like chums. Like pals. That's what we are. Yes," and this time she hiccupped.

"Then advise me," he said. "Give me some help. Somehow."

"Ahhh, help. Yesh. Help. H.E.L.P. I see what you mean. I am a friend so I help. Yes indeed." She closed her eyes in thought.

He stared at her dubiously. After a few moments he enquired, "Are you asleep?"

She opened her eyes. "Not a bit of it, I was meditating. I

meditate a lot. Well, I don't know a great deal about the *Bon*. I don't even shop there. But aren't there amulets, cures or something?"

"Yes, but they none of them seem to be useful really. They seem to involve spiders and toads and stuff a good deal of the time, and wearing amulets of precious stones. It's not practical."

"Ah," she said, "and we must be practical. Have you thought of apologizing?"

"What?"

"Apologizing," she enunciated clearly. "Ringing up and saying sorry."

"Yes, but I don't know what to say. I did try, though. I said 'I'm the ill-mannered person who laughed at a joke at your expense the other night and I am phoning to express my . . . ' and he rang off."

"Ahhh," she said. And then, "What time is it?"

He looked at his wrist. "Oh, I forgot." He pulled up his right trouser leg, and consulted the watch on his ankle. "Nine-thirty," he said.

"Then go round personally. The restaurant will shtill be open for bushi, businesh, business—it's the damned shibillants," she explained. "My teeth are the wrong shape or something. Maybe if I had another drinkie."

He ignored her request. "But if I go out like this—I mean with odd socks—and I don't know what else—well . . ."

"Jusht the thing," she said. "He'll let you off the hook onsh he shees you looking like that."

"Will he?" he asked eagerly.

"Give it the old try," she urged. "Put on what you fancy. Put on a lampshade inshtead of a hat. Leave off your trousers."

"They won't let me in."

"I'll come with you. You can hide behind me 'til we're safely inside. We could have a little late shupper," she added. "If a girl can't get one thing she must get another."

"You're a pal," he said.

"Yesh, a pal. Thatsh what I am. One for the road?"

"You know where it is," he said, and she went into the kitchen.

"Jusht a little one," she said as she poured, and then poured some more. "I'm a lush," she told the bottle and giggled. "Here's to frushtration!" she added and drank the toast. Her hair had fallen over one eye. She swept it back impatiently. "Onwardsh," she said firmly and only brushed the doorpost a little as she returned to the living room.

He emerged from the bedroom and stood awkwardly in front of her. He wore a tuxedo, a vivid Hawaiian shirt, and a pair of woolly slippers. His socks were still odd.

"That should do it," she told him, "that shertainly should do it. You're really very imaginative, when you try."

"It wasn't imagination," he said gloomily. "It's just what I felt compelled to put on."

"Then shall we go?" she enquired. "My car or yoursh?" She bit her lip and frowned. "That reminds me of something, but no matter."

"This is going to be fun," she said, leaning a little against him as he drove. "Don't you adore fancy dress parties?"

"No, and move away, will you?"

"I went as Beauty and the Beast once. I mean I went as Beauty and he was the Beast. He was very hairy," she said, "and horny," she added, chuckling.

He pushed her away again. "This is the place. Are you sober enough to manage it?"

"Absolutely," she said with some hauteur, and they entered the restaurant.

She only lurched a little on her way to the table in the far corner of the restaurant, and her voice had almost lost its slur when she responded to the polite enquiry as to whether or not they would have something from the bar. "I would very much like a drink. A double scotch on the rocksh," she said.

"Don't you think . . . ?

"No," she said. "Definitely no. I don't think at all. Drink-not-think is the word tonight." She hit the wine glass with her fork. It made a pleasing sound. She hit it again.

"Stop that. People are looking."

"Of course they are, who wouldn't?" Then, with a little giggle, she sang, not quite as softly as she might, "What do we say to the One-eyed Riley."

"You must eat something."

"I intend to. I intend to eat a great deal. Something Hawaiian I think," and she cackled with laughter.

He looked round him nervously. "The manager hasn't seen us yet." She nodded vigorously and the hair fell over her eyes once more. She brushed it away and reached for the drink that had just arrived.

"Are you ready to order, sir?" enquired the waiter.

"If the lady is ready," he replied.

The lady looked up. "He wants to see the manager."

"The manager is occupied at present, Madam, but I will inform him of your wishes. In the meantime, perhaps the potage du jour?"

"Yes, but first a plate of hors d'oevres. I like to nibble," she explained with a leer.

The waiter remained impassive. "And will the gentleman nibble also?"

"No," she said. "He never nibbles. Not even a little bit. He's a non-nibbler."

"Very well, Madam," said the waiter and left them.

She smiled brightly. "Thish ish fun, a fun evening. Almost more fun than . . ." her voice trailed off. "Where was I?"

"You were having fun, which is more than I am. Where is that damn manager?"

"Don't say damn," she warned him. "Mustn't shay damn. Nice manager. Kind manager. Manager with the *Bon*." She hit her wine glass with the fork once more. He winced. "I'm ringing for the manager," she explained. "Ring a ding ding." And she picked up the fork again.

"The manager is behind you," he hissed.

"Ah, sho he is." She craned round to look up at him. "You have a wall-eye!" she told him.

The manager inclined his head. "Yes, Madam, I do. I also wear odd socks. I am a somewhat odd person." He smiled. "And your friend," he commented, "seems equally odd."

"Yesh, he is, he does, he am," she told him firmly, "and itsh not fair. He didn't sing it. He laughed at the singinger, thatsh all."

Her companion said urgently, "I came here tonight to apologize and to ask if you could—if you are responsible of course—if you could, well,—I mean, look at me!" His voice rose in a squeak.

"Most unfortunate," said the manager gravely. "Just occasionally I am unable to control my feelings. It is really very tiresome."

"It's more than tiresome," he yelped—"it's infuriating—it's making me a laughing stock."

"I do understand," said the manager. "May I suggest a la Carte and the top of the menu, with a bottle of our most distinguished wine?"

There was a short silence. The girl gave a little hiccup. "I see," said her companion slowly, "I see."

"Yes," said the manager.

"Wheee!" the girl commented. "Wheee! It'sh a great town on the old time tonight." She frowned, puzzled. "Old town tonight," she corrected herself.

Her companion sighed heavily. "Whatever you say," he groaned.

"You will not regret it, Sir," the manager told him.

They sat there in silence for some moments, and then the girl rose to her feet. She did not stagger. "I'm just going to the powder room to freshen up. The meal will be perfectly splendid, I assure you. Splendidly, stupendously, sensually, satisfying—in all respects."

"You're not slurring."

She smiled. "It's my teeth. They're all behaving properly again. I can't have been drunk at all, can I?" And then, "I've a terribly hard head. That, at least, is what Daddy tells me. Doesn't he run a wonderful restaurant?"

Ah Freedom

*Y*ES, YES, I'M ALL ORGANIZED. *Don't worry. Have a good journey. Bye-bye. Bye-bye.*

Well, they're off. I'm alone. For the whole splendid weekend I'm alone. I can watch what I like on the TV, play all the records loud, especially those she hates, stay up all night if I feel like it. I'm my own man. In an empty house. Good old house. You and me are going to get on fine. It's a whole new relationship, do you realize? Time to get reacquainted. Hello house. Hello fridge. What have you got for me, my sweet? She said she'd stocked you up. And so she has! My, my, my! I'm going to do pretty well this weekend. Now I really must wander, case the joint as it were. Hello living room! Lord, but you look big. Bigger than before. Maybe you've expanded since she left. I feel a bit expanded myself, a bit released. No, not a bit, a lot. I could do a dance, couldn't I! Nobody to see me, after all. Tum-ti-tum-ti-tum. I could even sing. But what? 'Dr-i-ink tooo mee O-o-o-nly with thine eyes, and I will . . .' Why on earth that one? Hardly appropriate would you say? Still, what's appropriate? Appropriate shmappropriate. Hard to pronounce that. Still, onwards.

Funny climbing stairs to nobody for no reason. Let's be sneaky though. Let's look in here. Let's be a spy. What can I find out that I shouldn't? Sherlock Holmes faced with the abandoned room of a teenager: 'Ah Watson, you may easily deduce from the entangled pile of underwear in the armchair that the child left home in a hurry.' Wrong deduction, Holmes. She'd leave it like that if she'd had a month of Sundays to get away. Good grief, is she reading *that*? I haven't read it myself even. Let's see. "The first manifestation of paranormal activity in any environment should lead immediately to   a consideration of the significant psychological factors in the . . . ." Oh Lord, I can't bear it! Anyway, she's probably not really reading it. Not really. I didn't know she collected pot animals. There must be—yes—I make it twenty-three. They look like they came out of tins of cocoa or something. No, they don't do that anymore. You're out of date. But why didn't I know? There's lots I don't know. But I'm finding out, aren't I? This is positively exciting. The spy in the house. I ought to have a magnifying glass.

But press on. There's more yet. Our bedroom now. And her chest of drawers. Sticks a bit, this one. Tug. Tug. Oh. Well, thank God there was nothing breakable in it. All underwear. My God, I've never seen this one. It must be donkey's years old. Looks like the twenties anyway. Flapper days, or so they say. Funny term. Flap, flap, flap. Like penguins walking. 'Have you ever seen a pengwe-e-en wa-a-lking? Well I have!' I have, too. In the zoo. Remember that? Funny how there's never enough room to put things back in once they're out. Would she notice if I slipped a couple somewhere else? Answer, yes. Maybe if they were folded a bit. Think of all those stories and movies in which people search rooms thoroughly, looking for the gun or the secret papers and leave everything just as it was before, and nobody knows. Except Sherlock of course. 'A man searched this room, Watson.' 'How ever do you know?' 'Elementary, my dear Watson, no woman would ever fold a skirt this way. Therefore a man must have been in this room.' But he never really said 'Elementary, my Dear Watson,' did he? And don't they say he knew nothing about women? Well, I know something about women, and I'd better damn well get all this stuff back in the right drawer.

Another drawer? Well just one, a little one. I'm sounding like a boozer. Just a little one. Well, it is a bit addictive, just a bit. Take it easy this time. Oh, I see—letters. Well, there's a limit. I can't look at letters. Can't you? Oh, go on. All right just a peek then, just a little one—there I go again. The handwriting looks . . . it's mine. Good grief. They're my own letters. Well, I can read my own letters, can't I? They're my copyright after all. Just one maybe to remind me . . . I wish I hadn't done that. It was so long ago. And surely I was, we were . . . oh dear . . . one should never look back. Not ever. I think maybe I'll give up on this. Down to the living room, again, put on a record or something. What's that soap opera she never lets me watch? That's not fair. She'd let me watch anything. She'd just be a bit, well, surprised. And maybe feel sort of let down. 'The Loves of our Lives' wasn't it? 'Oh Henry, I thought you were going with Joyce tonight, so I invited David round. It doesn't mean anything, of course . . .' and so on and so on. But they're all very—what's the word? nubile—aren't they! But who cares! I don't. I certainly don't. In fact I must give up on all this wandering around, and make the most of this freedom.

I must do some work. Yes, work. I can really get down to it today and tomorrow. I could work all night if I felt like it. Right. Now, into the study. Here we are, here's the typewriter. Here's the paper. No problem. Oh, but I'd better put the answering service on, or I'll be interrupted, you can bet on it. And all the calls will be for her or Jennifer. Why on earth did we call her Jennifer? She isn't one at all. She's more—what can I say—Vivian. I don't know why Vivian. It just seems to fit, that's all. Vivian. Vivacious Vivian. Viv. Oh no, I pity any man who married a girl called Viv. That's almost Oscar Wilde isn't it? Ah, I knew it would ring before I got to it. It always does.

Hello. No, I'm afraid she's not in. She's away. Try her again on Monday. Can I take a message? Oh, hang on, I have to find a pencil. Where does she keep the damn things? Christ, it's broken. Ah, here's one. And paper. Loose sheets. *Yes, yes, Maybelline called to say . . . Excuse me just a moment . . .* this bloody paper slithers around like a mad thing . . . *Say what? Oh, that she called. All right I'll tell her that. And would she call back. Yes, yes. She will, I'm sure. Yes. Goodbye.*

Switch it on then, quick. Right. That's done. Now, to work. But, still, maybe a little drink. Just a little one. No, dammit, who's watching. Who cares? A big one. Scotch. On the rocks. Hello fridge. Got any ice, have you? Good old fridge. Damn it, that's the bell. Who the heck . . . ?

Yes? No I'm sorry but I'm not interested. No, I haven't read it. Well, I'm not religious. Look, I really am not interested. Why don't you call back when my wife's in. I really don't know if she's been saved or not. I never asked her. Goodbye. Have a good day.

That was mean. And stupid. They'll come back and tell her I told them to. 'It was a slip of the tongue' I'll say. No, better make sure I answer the door. What about a notice, like the ones they used to have? 'No Hawkers.' They're hawkers surely. 'Excuse me,' they should say, 'I'm hawking God.' And I could say 'Tradesmen at the back entrance please!' Or maybe just 'Beware of the Dog' would do. Or 'My Lion eats Christians.' Perhaps 'Nero lives here.' But they probably never heard of Nero. Except Nero Wolfe, no, they don't read that sort of stuff, I'm sure. I can't see it. They probably settle down of an evening with a recording of the Salvation Army Chorus or the Mormon Tabernacle Choir and read pamphlets aloud to each other and rehearse prayers. Maybe they rehearse other things too. Like smiling. They study toothpaste ads, that's it. 'Oh look at that one, Zachariah—look how she lifts her chin when she does it—and that air of confidence—and the way she looks you straight in the eyes.' 'Yes, Hepzibah, but her garments. They're not, well, that of a saved person exactly!' 'No, but the smile! We can learn from the breed without the law, Zachariah.' Breed without the law. That's Kipling. Not their cup of tea. I bet they never kipple at all.

Well, it's an old joke, I know, but the old ones are the good ones as the actress said to Methusaleh . . . . Sheesh! It must be the drink. My mind's going. Back to the study. Back to the typewriter. Now, where was I? Ah yes. Chapter fourteen. 'Roger idly picked up the newspaper from the front porch and the headline blazed out at him.' Jeezus, I must have been having a bad day when I wrote that. 'Blazed,' indeed. And 'idly.' Nobody can pick up a newspaper from the step idly. You have to bend right down, and grunt a bit, and on winter days it's either sodden with rain or blown apart with sheets all over the laurel bush. And this tale is set in the winter too. In a grim November. But that reminds me, what with all the fuss of getting them off on their weekend I haven't even glanced at the paper. I'll just do that thing. Freshen my glass and do that thing. Why not? I've time. I've all the time in the world. Well, until Monday. But Monday is a long way off. A very long way. What was that book? The Long Weekend? The Lost Weekend? No, that was a movie. Ray Milland. Drinking. Like me. Maybe I'm going to lose my weekend too. No, that's not my style. 'Never drink alone' they say. A bit stupid really. I mean when you're alone as I am alone . . . isn't that a quotation too? Don't think about it. When you're alone as . . . he . . . . To hell with it. But one thing is true. Never drink without eating. Not ever. So—good old fridge—cheese, I think. A big block of it all neatly plastic wrapped. Damn the thing. You can't tear it open unless you're Hulk Hogan or maybe a raccoon, but I'd like to see either of them cope with this joker. Scissors. That's the ticket—but no—she has a method. You just take a big knife and cut half an inch off the end, right through everything. Right? Here we go. Good. Now you find a baggie.

Baggie, Baggie, Baggie, where are you? Ah, I see, you little darlings, tucked away behind the twist ties, the aluminum foil, the empty paper bags, the oven mitts, the corkscrew, the tin opener and God knows what else. But they're the big ones! You could put complete cows in these. No small ones! Of course not. Naturally. Well, to hell with it. And crackers. Ah yes, crackers. But you can't use the knife on these. It's brute strength or nothing. And getting your finger in just the right place to . . . ouch . . . there goes the finger nail. Now I need the scissors. But they can wait. Cheese, crackers, and scotch. A mid morning snack. Time for a little snackerel.

And the news. Well, this time, this blessed time I get to the funnies and the horoscope first. Page what? Ah, yes, here we are. Why on earth they call them funnies I'll never know. Here's a young woman crying because she's spotted her husband talking to someone with unnaturally high cheek bones and black hair at the country club dance. Here's a cat clawing its master for having insulted it—both very funny creatures; you can tell that from their bulging eyeballs. Time for a thoughtful essay on the incidence of glaucoma and other eye disorders in the funny papers. Think about Orphan Annie! Here is a small round child asking its mother why daddy says the newspaper is bull. Daddy's right, mind you! And, oh Lord, that dreadful man with a face like a claw hammer is hitting his potato-headed son with a sausage. Someone ought to write a letter to the paper about it. Well, let's look at the letters. Maybe someone has. Oh no they haven't. But here's a character telling me that children today are pampered and that when he went to school he walked seven miles each way and carried a hot roast potato in a sock to keep his hands warm on the journey and to serve as lunch. I wonder how he kept warm on the way home? He must be ninety-three at least to remember that, which I suppose is possible in this city.

All things are possible in this city, even belief in experts' reports. Here's an expert telling us that recent studies show that if you live in a city you stand a great deal better chance of being murdered than if you live elsewhere. He has percentages on it. Our grandparents and great grandparents knew that. So did the Jews. 'Don't go to Sodom or Gomorrah, child,' they said. 'You'll get yourself killed.' And they were. By God himself. All of them. Except Lot. And his wife got changed into a pillar of salt. Experts tell us that if we eat too much salt our veins and arteries will harden. Maybe that's what it means really . . . . It's a dietary thing. Who was it died of a surfeit of lampblack? No, I'm thinking of Dickens. Why the Dickens am I thinking of Dickens? And why do we use Dickens like that?

Look, this is ridiculous. A quick peek at the horoscope and back to Roger on the doorstep. Let's see. 'Your financial situation is due to improve. Concentrate on creative and imaginative projects. You will receive a message from Virgo.' Well that's almost right. She's Virgo and she said she'd ring me when she got off the ferry. As for creative and imaginative—well, back to Roger and chapter fourteen. 'Roger bent down, heavily, and retrieved the newspaper from the far corner of the porch. It had blown apart and he grunted as he gathered it together. It was only when he had retrieved the last sheet that the headline caught his eye.' Stop! Stop! Stop! 'Caught his eye' is dreadful. A cliché. 'He saw the headline.' Now what the devil was the headline? 'Small earthquake in Peru. Not Many Dead'? Didn't that win a competition for the most boring newspaper headline once upon a time? And then there was one, wasn't there, for the most splendid typo. 'The Queen pissed over Westminster Bridge.' But stop wandering. The headline. Ah, yes. 'Ferry Disaster. Many Drowned.'

Why did I think of that? There hasn't been a ferry disaster in years, and, after all, she's insured. Careful she is. Travel insurance always. Flight insurance invariably. Aspirin, Tylenol, Antihistamine, Elastoplast, Antacid all in her purse. A walking dispensary. 'Don't worry, soldier, my wife can deal with your shattered leg. She carries splints and tourniquets wherever she goes. She is also expert at the kiss of life.' The kiss of life. That's what they ought to call scotch. Kissing the bottle—isn't that an expression for it? 'He's been kissing the bottle.' Better than sloshed, pissed, stoned, smashed, blotto, or those great phrases, drunk as a loon, drunk as a fiddler's bitch, half seas over, three sheets to the wind. Which reminds me. Just another little one. It stimulates the imagination. Doesn't do a damn thing for the typing but it stimulates the imagination. 'Concentrate on imaginative and creative projects' it said. 'Yes, that's what the man said. He said that.' Dialogue by William

Faulkner after Raymond Chandler, *The Big Sleep.* I love titles.
Wish I could think of them. 'The Ferry Disaster.' No. 'The Ferry
Fury.' But what could that be? A creature from the deep, reaching
up over the car deck, its huge tentacles sliming around her, Jenni-
fer screaming, the ship's siren going full blast . . . . Look here,
there's no ferry in this novel. All in suburbia. Superb suburbia.
Superbia. Where the superb people live. 'How simply superb!
What a simply superb house!' 'Well of course it *is* superbia.'

Actually it's a bust. I've never been so bored with any book I've
written. Bore yourself with a book! Buy this Book of Boredom. A
book for bedtime. Wasn't that a radio series once? Those lively
mellifluous voices. 'Henry has discovered that Sheila is going out
with David, and is angry and jealous. They confront each other in
the shopping mall's parking lot. Now here is chapter fourteen read
for you by . . . .' What's wrong with fourteen? It's not unlucky.
Well, not for everyone. Fourteen is a hell of a number really,
though. The sound of it even. Fooooourteeeen. Like two notes on
a trumpet. The final sound of *The Last Post.* I wish it *were* the last
chapter. She often reads the last chapter before she should. Can't
bear not to know if it turns out all right. Will the heroine survive
the ferry disaster? There I go again. She's on the ferry now,
anyway. Safely on her way, or I'd have heard. No news is good
news. Maybe there's something on TV. The News Channel. Why
not have a glance. Leave Roger stooping over his headline. Freeze-
frame him. Is that the expression? 'Freeze-frame.' Why do I think
of the Titanic? Ah yes, icebergs. But there are no icebergs in the
Straits of Georgia. There could be, though. The icecap is melting,
they say, and gradually the sea level will rise, and sooner or later the
prairies will be a huge sea, and the rockies an archipelago.

Well, that news isn't much. Just the usual death and destruction,

and another toothpaste ad. I wonder if they're looking in. 'Oh,
Zachariah, look at that Colgate smile. Do you think I should get
my teeth fixed?' A thought there. The relationship between salvation and tooth care. Brush your teeth and find God. Teeth and the
Truth. Floss and the Faith. Smile for Salvation. Oh God, but this
house is empty.

Pull yourself together. You have lots to do. Even apart from
chapter fourteen. Just for a start you could take the garbage out. In
one of those bags that look like they're made of seaweed. Perhaps
they are. Full fathom five thy garbage lies . . . how does it go . . . ?
'Nothing of it but doth change into something rich and strange.'
'Strange' is right. 'Rich' too, really. This has a smell that's both.
Where are those twist ties? Ah, here they are, tucked away, hiding
under the baggies. Ouch. Why do they leave sharp points like that?
Well, they didn't. It's a used one. Used and re-used. She's thrifty that
way. 'I've goo-t a woo-mmmaaaan keraaaaazyie to save; sheeee's
thrifty that waaaay . . . .'

Funny how the tin near the bottom of the bag always has a sharp
corner and hits your ankle. Especially as all the tins these days are
round. Not like the old bully beef tins of my youth. Mind you there
are sardine tins, come to think of it. Remember playing sardines?
Six people under one bed. Peas in a pod rather than sardines. All
oil. In the oil of excitement? Or maybe the tomato. I prefer the
tomato myself. Those lovely little red smears and globules. But
how to get them out without breaking them, especially the one in
the corner? And rolling that key so that it doesn't go askew. Life is
full of difficulties. Of course she makes light of them. Amazing
woman. She can even open cereal packets without swearing. There's
character for you.

I don't know why that TV is still on. I guess it's company of a kind, though who needs that kind of company at halfpast noon of a summer day? I should turn it off and go out. She's always telling me to go out. 'Enjoy the sun,' she says. What's to enjoy? It just shines and makes you sweaty and if you take off your clothes it fries you. Fried. I forgot that one. Fried. Boiled. Crocked. Hammered. Juiced. Well I'm not. Not yet, anyway. I could stand another little one while I make lunch.

What's for lunch, fridge, old darling. My shiny white darling. I see she's left me sandwiches. The working man's lunch. In plastic baggies. Small baggies. So that's where all the small ones went! I must save them for the cheese. Turkey loaf. Ah well. Times change. Letter to the paper. 'The working man today is pampered. When I was a boy we went to work with a hot potato in a sock, or a chip buttie.' Nobody knows what a chip buttie is nowadays. A french-fry sandwich doesn't sound the same at all. And what ever became of bread and dripping? Too salty, they say. It will turn your veins to stone. Or salt. Lot's wife again. I wish there was something on earth that one could eat without the spectre of Death leering over your shoulder with an alarming grin. Death is a dietitian. Now there's a title for you. I'd better make a note of it. But someone's probably used it already. It must be maddening sometimes. All the good titles are gone. Gone with the wind, as the actress said to the stomach specialist. Joke. I'm making jokes. I must be drunker than I thought. Why do I only make jokes when I'm drunk? Why do I get drunk when people tell me jokes? She never tells jokes. She tries, but she never makes it. Doesn't forget the punch line, mind you, she remembers that. It's the lead-up she forgets. 'Well, I can't remember just how it begins, but . . . .' Punchlines afloat on nothingness. On rafts of nothingness . . . . Like shipwrecked ferry passengers.

Not a bad sandwich actually. Not bad at all. 'Dear Sir, spare a thought for the deprived who are obliged to take chip butties to work for their lunch. Why should the rich have all the turkey sandwiches?' A chicken in every pot. There's a laugh. Just think of it. One chicken. I wonder if he intended to give one out to everyone when that war was over? 'Queue up here for your chicken,' carrying your pot? Perhaps some people had more than one pot. 'Five chickens here. This is a five pot family.' There's another one—potted. Canned. Bottled. Stewed. And you forgot Drunk as a Lord. Lords probably had a whole lot of pots. 'Five hundred chickens for the Marquis of Stoke on Trent. He lives in the potteries.'

Now what about dessert? We used to call it pudding, or the sweet. Now it's the dessert. Just 'dessert.' We get our just desserts. Do we really, and what would be my just dessert? Maybe a hangover, the way things are going? Certainly not. Did Lot's wife get her just desserts, simply for looking back? Looking back is always a bit dangerous. Think of Euridice, wasn't it, though she didn't turn to stone. She turned into a myth. Myth Euridithe. Or wouldn't she by Mythtreth? We don't use that word any longer. Confusing. Lover seems to be the word, and when Sheila says, 'I think Henry has a lover' you don't know if it's Joyce or James. And then there's 'Gay.' 'You're very gay tonight.' You can't say that any longer. 'Toujours Gai' said Mehitabel, hardly a lesbian cat. They used to name girls Gay once upon a time. I don't suppose they do now. And what about John Gay, the Gaiety Girls, Gay Paree . . . ? The language is going to rack and ruin. It's going to hell on a handcart. Euridice didn't have a handcart. She just walked. Didn't even take the ferry across the styx. Well, she's on a ferry, heading for the sticks you might say. Or the boonies. But she should have

got there by now. To the Other Side. That's another word for it.
The other side. There are songs about that too. No, no more
singing. She wouldn't like it. Nobody likes my singing. Understandable I suppose. But also unforgivable. It is such a freedom. I
feel so free when I sing. Free as the air I'm singing. Or trying to. 'O
for the la-a—ss with the de-lic-ate air, the deli, deli, deli, deli-cate
ayyer, I love the laaaass with the delicate air.' She isn't particularly
delicate though, and no longer a lass. Alas no lass. No lass alas. A
lasst chapter. Perhaps I could make chapter fourteen the lasst
chapter. It's the last one I'll ever write, I'm sure of it. Roger is going
to stay on that damn porch stooping over his newspaper forever,
turned suddenly into stone, or salt, for looking back at a headline.
'Ferry Struck by Hand of God.' No, it can't have been. For one
thing it's time it had docked. On the Other Side.

There we go again. 'Someone is trying to make contact from the
Other Side. Does anyone here have a name beginning with a P . . .
a man . . . Peter perhaps?' What a name! Peter Perhaps. Mary
Maybe. Pauline Possible. Daphne Doubtless. Sarah Certainty. A
whole cast list there. A Restoration Comedy. Comedy needs to be
restored. Think of the sit-coms on TV. No don't. It will only
depress you. Television Sitcoms drive me to drink. In fact they're
drifing me there right now. Just another little one. Just a snort, a
shot, a snifter, a quick one, a peg . . . and then, well, what if I do get
swacked, stinking, sozzled? What if? I'm free this weekend. Free to
do just what I damn well please. Free as the air I'm not allowed to
sing. Free, even, to ignore chapter fourteen.

Ah, there it goes, that damn phone—what's this? 'We are
terribly sorry we are unable to come to the phone . . .' Oh yes, my
God how dreadful it sounds, like a . . . *Yes, yes, I'm here* . . . . 'At the
sound of the beep . . . .' *All right, yes* . . . . *Sorry, Dear, I left the*

machine on . . . . Yes, I'm fine . . . . Great of you to call . . . . So you've got over the great water successfully have you? . . . Of course I wasn't worried. Just starting chapter fourteen . . . . Yes dear, yes, dear, yes dear, I'll deal with it. Yes dear, I took out the garbage like you said. Have a good time . . . . Of course I'm not . . . you know I hate drinking alone . . . . Yes, yes, I'm all organized. Don't worry. Have a good journey the rest of your trip. See you Monday. Bye-bye. Bye-bye.

Well, she's all right. Thank God. And now the weekend can really start. A free weekend. A weekend to do anything I like. A weekend to write in, free from interruption. Two whole days free for chapter fourteen. Lots of time. I can relax now. In fact I will. I think I'll have a nap. Just a little one. Ah, freedom.